8.8.23

Emily's Evil

G000135983

by Geoffrey Sl

Text copyright © 2019 Geoffrey Sleight

All rights reserved

This is a work of fiction. Names, characters and events in this narrative are fictitious. Any resemblance to persons living or dead is purely coincidental.

All deception in the course of life is indeed nothing else but a lie reduced to practice, and falsehood passing from words into things.

Robert Southey

CHAPTER 1

FROM family talk in hushed tones during my childhood, I knew strange events had taken place at my grandfather's country house, but little did I know on receiving an invitation to join him there, how frighteningly that past would come to life.

I'd not long been demobilised from the army at the end of the second world war, and returning from overseas to the bombed, rubble strewn streets around my home in London, the invite to his country retreat was welcome.

I remembered staying at his house with my parents as a child. That I'd woken one night to see standing at the end of my bed a young girl in a red frock and blue ribbon in her fair hair.

"This used to be my room," she said, then disappeared.

I got out of bed and called to my parents who were in a nearby bedroom.

"There was a girl in my room," I told my father, as he peered out and saw me. He took me back and looked around the room.

"I think you were dreaming Tom. Best to get back in bed and go to sleep again." He reassured me all was well.

While the vivid memory of that moment faded over the years, it always remained at the back of my mind. I knew I wasn't asleep when I saw her, and there was certainly no young girl living there at the time.

My grandfather sometimes came to stay with us for a while at my parents house in London, and I always loved his friendly company. But I sensed my father did not warm to him. Had they had a rift? I didn't know. In my tender years of childhood, grown-ups didn't convey their family feelings to the young.

Reaching adulthood, my job as a solicitor's clerk with the prospect of qualifying and starting my own practice was rudely interrupted by war service. By the end of it, years had passed since I'd last seen my grandfather. He was now in his mid-seventies, and as well as wanting to be re-united with him, it dawned on me that in the not too distant future the opportunity to see him again would be lost with his passing.

When I think back now to the events that happened on my visit, it might have been better for the past to have remained in the past. But hindsight is a wonderful thing.

After packing a suitcase, I set off for the 115-mile drive to my grandfather's house just outside a village called Bramthorpe in Dorset. With back pay from military service, I'd bought a Ford 8 car, now pride of possession, but the rutted roads as I neared my destination nearly shook me and the car to pieces.

This was remote countryside, but with outstanding views spanning meadows and hilltop woodlands. Vitalisingly peaceful and refreshing from the horrors of war.

The approach to the house was down a narrow lane so deeply potholed I feared the car would finally shatter. The forecourt of the house must have once been perfectly paved, but was now cracked and sunken virtually all over.

It was a relief to get out of the car and ease my still shaking muscles and bones.

Glancing at the property, it had all the evidence of once being owned by a wealthy family. A grand home with pitched eaves, bright white render and tall sash windows boasting the structure's presence. Now the render was stained and dirtied with time, the windows rotted and flaking and the roof tiles broken in places with many of them missing.

I had no recollection of the building's look from childhood memory beyond knowing it was a huge house inside, with long corridors on the ground and upper floors. The one on the first floor was particularly memorable, containing the bedroom where I'd seen that girl appear in the night.

I looked around at the large landscaped gardens, and images of my grandfather playing games with me came flooding back. As I recalled the memory, the front door opened and he came out of the house.

"Tom," he greeted with a cheerful smile. "I'd hardly recognise you. It's been so many years."

I was a teenager of fourteen when we'd last met eleven years earlier at my parents' home in London. He had changed too, now with just thin wisps of grey hair each side of his head, but the hair loss compensated by a full, silvery beard. His friendly manner, however, remained unchanged.

"Don't see many cars round here," he said, inspecting my Ford. "Quite the man about town now I see." His remark demonstrated that civilisation still had a lot of scope to make inroads in this deeply rural setting.

Inside the house more long forgotten memories returned. The wide, wood panelled hallway, the chequered black and white tiled floor and spacious winding stairway. Now though the setting seemed more neglected. Maybe it was ingrained dust and a slight mustiness in the atmosphere, but hard to compare with recollection from childhood.

"Leave your bag in the hall. Come and have some tea and cake with me before I show you to your room," my grandfather put his arm round my shoulders and led me into the dining room.

Yet more memory came back. The wood panelling, the long mahogany table that once must have hosted many guests for dinner. Even the same portraits of hunting dogs and horses hung on the walls. But again the room looked scarcely cared for, a bit dusty, unpolished and neglected.

"Sit down and take the weight off," he smiled. "I'll fetch the tea and cakes."

As he left through a door that connected to the kitchen, I remembered the table used to have a full set of chairs along each side. My father had commented on the visit years back, 'Georgian chairs, they must be worth a fortune'. Now only three remained, grouped at one end. The place had obviously deteriorated a great deal since my last time there.

A few minutes later grandfather re-appeared with a pot of tea and cakes. We sat at the table and he asked after the family, my brother Alan, and mum and dad. Then he wondered how I'd coped with war service.

My memory of it was still raw, and I'd conditioned myself to looking forward rather than back.

"Lost some good friends during the final push in the desert," I told him, "I'll always remember them." He could see the experience had left an indelible mark on me, and guided the conversation away.

"Come on let's get you settled in your room," he said, after we finished our tea.

Mounting the steps leading to the first floor with its long corridors on each side, he led me to a room halfway down the left passageway.

"This will be familiar to you." He opened the door. It was. The very room where I'd stayed as a boy. The one where I saw the girl in the night. The memory had remained distant, but now for a moment I had an uneasy sense the girl was present. Invisible. Watching me. Swiftly I dismissed it as a silly memory briefly surfacing. If only it had stayed that way.

The room was virtually unchanged. The wood panelling, a large oakwood wardrobe, the chest of drawers, the window overlooking the forecourt and the same kerosene lamp on the bedside table. The lamp made me realise that like that earlier time, electricity still hadn't been installed in the house.

"Unpack your things and we'll go for a stroll in the garden. Then you can help me prepare dinner," he smiled, closing the door.

Four acres of garden extended around the property. Trees and shrubs dotted across the lawns and all looking in need of serious cutting and maintenance, unlike the neat, trim garden grounds I recalled. But I said nothing as we chatted on our walk.

"And do you have a young lady?" my grandfather enquired, after we'd talked a little more about the recent war, and food rationing that was still affecting the country.

His question took me by surprise, I wasn't expecting to be asked about my love life.

"Well I'm friends with a lady called Ruth," I told him. "We met when I returned from desert operations. She was in the women's auxiliary service and now lives not far from me. We go out for dinner occasionally. Nothing serious," I played it down.

My grandfather gave a knowing smile, realising my modest, slightly embarrassed account of the relationship revealed a deeper feeling I held for the woman. He left the subject alone.

Since he'd been direct in asking about my personal life, I decided that perhaps I should be direct too concerning the family gossip about the house, but always in hushed, indistinct tones. It had long frustrated me never knowing exactly what strange events had happened there in the past.

"Can you tell me about the family history here?" I asked. "Things happened, I'm told, but I've no idea what."

My grandfather stopped walking and stared for a moment through the gap in a row of trees towards a distant view of meadows.

"Your father and mother no doubt, an aunt or uncle, all talking in whispers," he answered me after a long pause. "I know there's gossip in the family." He paused again, then turned to me. "Very few of them really know what happened. But after dinner tonight, I'll tell you a bit about past events here."

His enigmatic reply intrigued me, but he said no more as we made our way back to the house.

Freshening up before helping him to prepare dinner was not entirely civilised. The only running water for the property came from an outside tap at the back. There was a small ablutions room down the corridor from my room with a basin, mirror and water in a jug. Another memory that vividly returned from childhood.

The kitchen had hardly changed either, remaining steeped in earlier times. I peeled vegetables while my grandfather filled a chicken with stuffing and then tipped coal from a bucket into the glowing opening of the large, black metal cooking range. A dresser I remember containing cutlery and cooking pots was still there, and shelves with jars of herbs and spices, except most of the jars were now empty of any contents.

I finished preparing the vegetables and offered to help with the cooking.

"No, I'll see to it now. You go and relax in the lounge. Or take another stroll in the garden while it's still light," he said. "I'll call you when it's ready."

I entered the hall and walked down the long corridor to the lounge at the end. Memory was fuzzier here. It was not a room I frequented as a boy. Adults only mostly.

Another dark wood panelled room, with grim looking men and women peering from gold framed portraits made the place look strictly uninviting. I presumed they were past family members.

A light brown chaise longue stood in front of the bay window overlooking the grounds at the rear of the house.

Unlike the bare wood floors in other rooms, a large oriental rug looking excessively worn lay underfoot.

One side of the room contained a large bookshelf, which mostly held works unfamiliar to me, weighty volumes of science, mathematics and physics. But a small section had a few mystery, detective and thriller novels.

I chose one at random and sat on the chaise longue to read it, but my mind couldn't concentrate and after a few pages I decided to go for another stroll in the garden. It was as if some intangible force was urging me on.

The day was starting to fade towards twilight when I stepped outside. Memories of being playfully chased around the garden by my grandfather when I was a boy reminded me of those halcyon days.

As I strolled in the peaceful surroundings, the corner of my eye suddenly caught sight of a figure a short distance away beneath a tree. I turned to look. A young girl stood there, perhaps no older than ten years, wearing a red frock and a blue ribbon in her fair hair. I backed away in shock. She was the girl I'd seen in my bedroom all those years ago. She smiled at me.

"It's been a long time since we last met, and now you're a grown man," she said. "I do hope you'll stay. There is so much I want to show you."

She remained smiling for a few more seconds, then disappeared.

Who was the girl? Had I really seen her? Was it my imagination? No, it was not. I was convinced the spectre had really been there, just as I remained convinced that I'd seen her in my bedroom all those years ago.

"Tom," I heard my grandfather calling from the house. The call hardly registered on me. I stood mystified by the vision I'd seen and the girl's words, 'there is so much I want to show you.' Show me what?

"Dinner's nearly ready," shouted my grandfather, unable to see I was about a fifty yards from the front of the house, standing behind a line of bushes. The second call shook me out of my trance.

"Coming," I replied.

He served the meal in the dining room, and was obviously a good cook, the chicken and vegetables prepared to perfection. But the vision and words of the girl continued to haunt me.

"Are you alright?" he asked after a while. "Looks like you have something on your mind."

"No, I'm okay," I said, finishing the meal and resting my knife and fork on the plate. I was reluctant to tell him what I'd seen. Although certain of the girl's appearance, I didn't want to give my grandfather the impression I had an overactive imagination. Even now I was beginning to doubt myself. Maybe some subconscious boyhood memory had resurrected itself in the setting of the house.

After dinner my grandfather invited me to relax with him over a glass of wine in the sitting room. Burning logs flickered in the fireplace, warming the chill evening air that now penetrated the old building.

As well as the glow of the fire, two kerosene lamps lit the room perched at each end of the mantelpiece, with two more on corner shelves. Several framed portraits of woodland pastures were hung on the walls. We sat in armchairs facing the fire.

"Glad you enjoyed the meal," he said.

"It was perfect."

"Good. I've had to learn a few culinary skills since my wife Mary died. She was an amazing cook."

I waited as my grandfather reflected on the past. I'd never known my grandmother. She had died a year or so before I was born.

"Strange events have happened in this house," he said, suddenly reviving from his thoughts. "I know there's been plenty of family gossip over the years."

For a second I was thrown, not expecting this turn of conversation.

"People went mysteriously missing from here. Family members and staff," he paused briefly, glancing at me.

"My father was a wealthy man back in earlier days. Did well from his stock market business investments. We had servants and a governess to educate me and my sisters," he said, taking a sip of wine.

"First a young man from the village went missing. Then the governess. A little time after that my sister Victoria disappeared." He took another sip.

"Of course there were village rumours, but there wasn't a proper police force like today. We had a village constable who also doubled up as one of two volunteer firemen, with nothing more than a shack to house the fire engine. Even that was only equipped with buckets and a small water tank." My grandfather smiled at the memory of such an inadequate set-up.

"The constable came here a number of times to look into the strange disappearances. But my father being a wealthy man had a much higher class status than a lowly policeman. The constable's enquiries amounted to him having a swift look round the house and grounds, and departing with much embarrassment at having the audacity to suspect that a wealthy man could ever be party to criminal activities." He grunted an ironic laugh at the memory, shaking his head.

I listened to him totally fascinated. It was all a revelation to me.

"A couple of years later, when I was sixteen, my father sent me away to naval college. He thought a naval career would be good for me. Make me a strong man. I loved it. Training ship exercises off the local coast at Dartmouth. I was set for the navy. Then at eighteen, I was called home. My mother had mysteriously disappeared. My father was distraught. So was I."

He gulped his wine at the memory, finishing the glass and reaching for the bottle between us on a small side table.

"Want some more?" he offered me a refill, but I'd hardly drunk mine, so entranced by his tale.

"In fact it destroyed my father. At about the same time his business investments had taken a turn for the worse, and he asked me to forget a naval career, but instead help him in a strategy to recover his investment losses." My grand-father grunted again at the memory.

"I had no skills in it. Money was bleeding away. We had to dispense with staff and a year later my father died. A broken man at the loss of my mother, who we both loved dearly, and the collapse of his business investments. Only two of us remained. Me and my younger sister Emily."

"That's heartbreaking," I said, learning of family life that was completely unknown to me, as well as my grandfather's suffering.

"All water under the bridge now," he said.

"Didn't you ever find out what happened to everyone who mysteriously disappeared?" I asked.

He turned his head to look at me, the gaze in his eyes steeped in the distant past, with no hint of an answer to my question. Then he stared at the fire again, continuing his tale.

"Emily and me had a little money left, but running a house this size, maintaining it without servants and paying for general building repairs was costly. Then I met your grandmother, Mary, whose father owned a local ironmongery store in the village. A little later Mary and I married. Her father also owned the local grocery store and sold the business to me at a preferential price. It earned enough for me and your grandmother, beautiful young woman she was, to live sparsely at this house. But we were happy."

He stood up and tossed another log from a bundle on the side of the fireplace into the glowing embers of the fire. Then settled again in the armchair.

"My sister Emily hated the prospect of me bringing my wife to live in the house with us. Shortly before my marriage she left, and I never heard from her again. The rest you know. Your father was born and lived here, helping me in the shop until he was eighteen, and then went on to get a job with an insurance company in London." He paused again, gathering his thoughts.

"When my wife's father died, I also took over the iron-mongery business. With income from both stores, Mary and me could live fairly comfortably here. But when Mary died, I sold the businesses and had enough money invested from the sales to just about get by. As you can see, the house is in need of restoration, and my old bones aren't up to the work."

We chatted a little while longer about other things. I felt he didn't want to reflect on the past any longer, though I re-mained curious about the strange disappearances of people at the house. Perhaps he would give me some answers on another day. I didn't realise at that moment the answers were going to horrifically impact on my life in ways I could never have imagined.

"I've made up a fire in your room, just set light to the firelighters," my grandfather took a box of matches from his pocket and handed them to me. "It should keep you warm through the night, and there are more logs on the side of the fireplace."

We collected a kerosene lamp each from the kitchen to see the way to our beds. The lamplight shadows darting around us as we climbed the stairway looked creepy, but I gave no hint of my unease, and my grandfather was prob-ably well used to this remote way of living.

At the top of the stairs we said goodnight, and he made his way to a bedroom on the opposite side of the landing to mine. Inside my room, there was a kerosene lamp burning on the dresser. I placed the one I held on the bedside table then lit the fire, which soon took the night chill from the air.

For a while I read a book I'd brought with me. A cosy glow from the fire began to give enough light for me to put out the kerosene lamps, undress and settle down between the sheets.

But the semi-darkness in the corners of the room started to give me the creeps again. The thought of that little girl appearing here when I was a boy started to obsess me. I'd been terrified a number of times in wartime conflict. This, however, was a different sense of fear. An unnatural sense of something lurking, watching. An intangible force to deal with.

I got out of bed and re-lit the lamp on the dresser to drive out the dark, feeling stupid for harbouring such fear as a grown man. Settling down again, the warmth from the fire helped to relax me, and gradually I slipped into sleep.

The sound of voices outside the room woke me. A man and woman talking. I looked at my watch on the bedside table. It was three in the morning. Surely a woman hadn't entered the house in the night, and the man's voice didn't sound like my grandfather.

I opened the door and looked along the corridor. On the landing at the top of the stairs stood a middle-aged man dressed in a dark suit and wing collar shirt. He was talking to a young woman wearing a blue jacket and cream bustle skirt.

"But Percy's been missing for three weeks now. He must have jilted me or something terrible must have happened to him," she sounded deeply distressed.

"My dear, we've searched everywhere for him. The village search party has also been unable to track him down. Perhaps he's been called away on business," the man attempted to comfort her. "Please Victoria, try to calm yourself."

"No father, I can't." The woman stormed off towards the corridor on the far side. The man began to descend the stairs, and the source of light that had lit the scene fell into darkness.

I grabbed the kerosene lamp from my dresser and ventured along the corridor to where I'd seen them. Everywhere around was silent. No sign of anyone. Then it dawned on me the woman was dressed in clothes that came from a former era. The nineteenth century. They were both ghosts. The realisation made be shudder.

Curious as I was to know about past events in this house, my resolve to stay here was fading. Life back in bombed and rubble strewn London was beginning to seem more attractive. But I couldn't just walk out on my grandfather. Maybe in a day or two I could tell him there was an urgent appointment I'd forgotten about. That I had to return home. Staying in this place was not turning out to be as peaceful as hoped.

Returning to bed, I laid awake for what seemed hours before dropping into some semblance of sleep.

CHAPTER 2

"BREAKFAST in ten minutes," my grandfather announced, knocking on the bedroom door. I woke feeling unrefreshed from the brief rest I'd managed, but got ready quickly and went downstairs to the dining room.

"I hope you like kippers," he said, placing the plate on the table. "We have an excellent fishmonger in the village and I got some in fresh yesterday before you arrived."

I did enjoy kippers, and with toast and tea began to feel much better.

"How was your night?" he asked, as we sat eating together.

Should I tell him about the strange encounter I'd seen on the landing? For the moment I said nothing. He might think me a bit odd. I was still trying to convince myself that what I'd seen had been a fantasy. Was I developing some latent psychosis that had been triggered by the traumas of my experiences in the war?

"I had a very comfortable night," was my reply, which seemed to please him. Then he told me of the plan he'd mapped for our day.

It began with a stroll to the local village Bramthorpe, half-a-mile away, to show me the ironmongery and grocery shops he once owned. He introduced me to the present owners who'd bought the stores from him some years earlier, and we chatted for a while before continuing down the high street past several more shops and terraced cottages lining each side.

"Good morning Mr Roberts," a man with thinning grey hair and peppery pencil moustache greeted my grandfather with a smile from behind the counter, as we entered the local post office which doubled as a newsagent store.

"Half an ounce of wine gums and the same with your mint humbugs please Toby," my grandfather ordered. The man took two jars from shelves filled with sweets behind him, weighed the gums and humbugs on scales, and tipped them into brown paper bags.

"My weakness Tom," grandfather smiled at me. "What's yours?"

I pointed to liquorice twists in a jar.

Strolling back to the house we enjoyed some of our treats, armed also with supplies of a fresh loaf and some cakes from the local baker.

"Do you like archery?" he asked.

"Never done it before," I answered. He was keen to introduce me to the art.

On a wide sweep of lawn he set up the target, and with two excellent bows and fine set of arrows, we spent much of the afternoon in competition after he'd shown me some basic techniques.

Of course, his expertise won the day. I was a novice.

"Used to win a lot of local competitions at this," he boasted proudly, before releasing another arrow to hit centre target.

My skill had been with a rifle and aiming grenades during the war. I was content to be unskilled at this pursuit, because it didn't result in any loss of life. I'd seen enough of that.

Late afternoon we packed up and returned to the house.

"I've a delicious beef joint for dinner," he said, while we drank tea and ate biscuits in the kitchen. I offered to help prepare it.

"No, you go and relax," he declined the offer. "There's plenty to read on the bookcase in the lounge. I'll be fine doing it."

With my uneasy night's sleep and an active daytime, I was glad for the chance to sit for a while. Settling on the chaise longue, I began reading the thriller novel I'd started last time I was in the room. Ten minutes must have passed when I began to feel the sensation of a presence near me. Looking up, the girl in the red frock I'd seen before was watching me from a few feet away. Her eyes sparkled with mischievous cunning.

"Follow me, I would like to show you something," she said. I remained seated, stunned by her sudden, silent appearance and wondering if I was just imagining the girl. But her image was still there.

"Come on," she said, beckoning. Curiosity compelled me to follow. She led me towards the kitchen. I expected to find my grandfather preparing our meal, but he wasn't present.

Instead, a well spread, middle-aged woman wearing a white mob cap and apron over her grey dress stood stirring the contents of a saucepan on the cooking range. Apart from the range, the kitchen appeared different, the walls of bare stone, dead pheasants and rabbits hanging forlornly from hooks on a sidewall, and a sturdy dark oak table in the centre of the room scattered with chopping and carving knives.

The cook tending to the saucepan turned towards us.

"Miss Emily. What brings you here?" she asked the girl. The woman seemed unaware of my presence. And that name? The name of my grandfather's sister. Could it be?"

"It's a very hot day Hetty. Do you think I could have a glass of lemonade?" the girl asked.

"Always after something, ain't you Miss Emily?" the cook smiled.

She took hold of a jug resting beside some glasses on a wooden work surface nearby and poured the drink into a glass.

"Thank you Hetty," Emily smiled back, taking the lemonade and beckoning me to follow her out of the kitchen.

We entered the hall and she led me along a corridor under the stairway to a door halfway down. With her free right hand, she lifted the side of her red frock and produced a key tucked into her underwear.

"I got this from father's study when he was taking his morning walk," she told me, inserting the key in the door lock and opening it. Inside were shelves filled with rows of bottles.

"The medicine cabinet," said the girl. She placed the glass in a space on one of the shelves and took down a bottle marked ARSENIC. Opening the bottle, she poured a generous quantity into the glass of lemonade.

"It's good for rheumatism and other ailments," she told me, "as well as unwanted pests."

I stared in amazement wondering what she was doing. The quantity she'd just poured into the glass would swiftly kill someone stone dead. She replaced the bottle, took the glass and locked the door, beckoning me to continue following her.

The end of the corridor led to a side door opening into the garden. When I'd come in from the garden earlier with my grandfather, the sky was darkening with a chill evening air. Now the sun shone brightly and the temperature was searing hot.

The girl I now knew as Emily made her way towards a tiled roof gazebo, where a man and woman were seated together on a bench inside. It was the first time I'd seen a gazebo in the garden. Emily stopped before approaching the couple.

"That man Percy Withenshaw is engaged to my older sister Victoria sitting with him," she said. "I know that he's untrustworthy. A deceiver. I've seen him going in and out of a house in the village where women of low moral virtue practise their trade. He will give my sister an unhappy life. I will not tolerate that." The girl's voice filled with anger at the thought. She began walking towards them.

"Emily, what do you want?" her sister Victoria snarled, annoyed at the intrusion. She wore a light yellow silk dress, with white lace ruffs on the sleeves, her brown hair tied in a bun. The man was dressed in a tail coat, crimson shirt with a yellow ruffled cravat and dark blue breeches.

"Father wants to see you in the drawing room," Emily told her.

"Why?" demanded Victoria.

"He wouldn't say."

The woman stood up, furious at being interrupted.

"Wait here Percy, I shall return shortly," she told her fiancée.

"Yes my love," he smiled, standing up at her departure.

When she'd left, Emily turned to Percy.

"While my sister's seeing father, there's something I'd like to show you," she said to the young man.

"And what is that Miss Emily?" he grinned patron-isingly, his black bushy moustache being the main feature of his otherwise uneventful long, thin face.

"You'll have to follow me. It's only a short distance away."

The man seemed happy to follow the girl in what ap-peared a bit of innocent fun.

I followed too, drawn by this extraordinary scene that appeared to be more vivid than a dream.

She led him to a wide spread of rhododendrons with a narrow gap near the centre, where she stopped.

"What is it you want to show me?" Percy asked.

"Do you believe in fairies?" Emily questioned him.

"I do, if you do," he replied, humouring her with another grin.

"This is the entrance to where they live," Emily pointed to the gap in the cluster. "You'll see them come out if you stand close and take a drink of my lemonade."

Ready to continue humouring the younger sister of his fiancée, Percy took hold of the lemonade glass that Emily held out to him, and took several gulps. He handed the glass back to her and began staring into the gap, continuing to play the young girl's game, and starting to pretend he could see fairies. But the pretence came to an abrupt halt. Within a few moments he broke into a cry of crippling agony, clutching his stomach and violently retching to throw out the arsenic poison. It was in vain.

As he bent double facing the gap, Emily gave him a hard shove, and his body toppled lifeless into the surrounding bushes to practically cover him from sight.

I could hardly believe what I was witnessing. Emily had murdered the man in cold blood.

"That's evil. You've killed him," I cried.

"He deserved it," she replied, no hint of emotion.

I could stand this ghostly nightmare no longer and wanted to return to the house. However, I remained locked into this strange past and found myself following Emily back to the gazebo. A few moments later Victoria returned.

"Father said he did not ask to see me," she was angry with her sister. "You were playing one of your nasty little jokes, weren't you?"

Emily gave an apologetic smile as if she was just having an innocent bit of fun. But Victoria's anger quickly turned to concern.

"Where's Percy?" she asked.

"He suddenly remembered he had a business appointment and had to leave. He said a carriage would be arriving soon in the village to take him into town," Emily lied.

"How rude!" Victoria's fury was now focussed on her fiancée. "I shall have words." She turned and stormed back towards the house.

I called after her, wanting to tell the woman the truth, but it was futile. In this setting I was the ghost, unseen and unheard to all except Emily.

Within moments the sky darkened into the late stage of twilight. The surrounds were just visible and I found myself standing near the spread of rhododendrons where deceased Percy had been cruelly murdered.

"Quickly Edward! Did you bring the rope from the garden shed?" Emily whispered urgently, standing beside the gap in the bushes.

"Yes," a boy called back approaching her. In the near darkness I could just about make him out. He seemed to be wearing a waistcoat over a white shirt and dark trousers. He looked a little taller and older than the girl.

"Why d'ye need the rope?" he asked, nearing her.

"Just come over here."

The boy followed to the gap, peering inside to see a shape half covered in leaves.

"It's a man! Is he drunk?" The youngster stepped back in surprise.

"No Edward, he's dead," said Emily, as if it was a perfectly normal announcement.

"No!" The boy's mouth dropped. "Who is it?"

"Percy. Victoria's fiancée."

"No! We'd better tell father," he was about to leave, backing away.

"Stay here!" Emily demanded.

"Why? We need to get help."

"Because I killed him with poison and we need to get rid of his body," Emily explained matter of factly.

"You're playing one of your games, aren't you? Percy and you are trying to fool me, aren't you?" the boy appeared relieved for a second.

"No, I've really killed him. He's really dead."

"Why?" The lad recoiled in shock.

"Because he's a bad man and would make Victoria unhappy."

"They'll lock you up in an asylum for the rest of your life," Edward became panic stricken.

"I know, that's why you've got to help me," Emily pleaded.

"How?"

"Tie the rope around his legs and we'll drag him to the old disused well."

Edward hesitated.

"Do you want me to be put away for the rest of my life? Or they might even hang me." Emily sounded fearful.

Reluctantly the boy knelt down, brushed the leaves away from Percy's body and tied the rope around his legs.

"Now help me to pull him to the well," Emily ordered.

Percy's dead weight was an immense challenge to them. It took some time to drag the body across the lawn in the near darkness, made slightly easier by the downward slope of the ground in their direction.

I witnessed the bizarre scene like a person detached from reality. Events unfolding that I was powerless to intervene and change. Daylight had slipped away, but a haze of moonlight now dimly lit the sky through a misty layer.

Gasping for breath under the strain of Percy's weight, they finally reached the round structure of a well. It was a feature that had been absent when I'd earlier strolled in the grounds.

Now they had a monumental struggle hoisting Percy's body up against the well, pausing several more times for breath. As the top of his body leaned lifelessly forward over the wall, both of them lifted his legs and heaved him into the opening. Several seconds passed before a distant splash echoed upwards. Percy was no more.

The youngsters sank to the ground resting their backs against the wall to regain their strength.

"You must never tell anyone what we've done," said Emily to her brother, getting up after her rest. "Because now you've helped me, they'd put you in an asylum or even hang you too."

The scene before me began to dissolve. For a moment I stood completely disorientated, wondering where I was. Then I became aware of standing beside the house near the front door.

My mind raced in confusion, coupled with the deeply troubling fact that my grandfather's first name is Edward. Was he that young boy I'd seen helping Emily to dispose of the body?

I made my way to the kitchen expecting to see my grandfather preparing the meal. Opening the door, the room appeared empty. A pot was simmering on the range and I could smell the aroma of beef cooking in the oven.

"Grandfather," I called, approaching the range, then froze in shock. He was laying unconscious face up on the floor. I stooped down beside him, fearing he was dead, and reached for his wrist. For a moment I could feel no pulse, then detected a very weak beat. He needed urgent medical help, but there was no phone in the house and I had no idea who was his doctor. I'd have to call for an ambulance from the village phone box.

With the track and road leading from the house so rutted, I could run to the village faster than it would take me to drive. Within ten minutes, and nearly out of breath, I reached the phone box in the high street, but it was out of order.

A light shone from the baker's shop across the road. I could see a man through the front window sweeping the floor and ran across to him, knocking frantically on the locked door.

"We're closed," he called back.

"Please help me! It's an emergency," I shouted.

The man stopped sweeping and unlocked the door.

"What's up?"

"My grandfather. He's very ill. He needs a doctor," I blurted breathlessly.

"Right, come in and wait here. I'll call Doctor Marsh. You're Mr Roberts' grandson aren't you?" I nodded. He recognised me from the visit I'd made earlier with grandfather.

The man disappeared behind a door, returning a minute later.

"I've called the doctor. His wife says he's out on a call, but she'll send him round. Probably half-an-hour."

"Can I get an ambulance for him? Take him to hospital?" I was worried any time delay could be fatal for the man.

"The doctor will be quicker. It'll take ages for an ambulance to arrive from the nearest town hospital," the baker advised. I had no option other than to take the advice.

"Thank you," I said hurriedly, quickly leaving to be back at my grandfather's side.

CHAPTER 3

THE DOCTOR finished examining my grandfather. I'd carried him upstairs to his bed after returning to the house.

"He needs to be in hospital," said Dr Marsh, packing his medical instruments back into a case. He looked at me sternly through gold rimmed spectacles under a head of neatly side combed grey hair.

"What's wrong with him? I asked.

"I think it's his heart. The injection I've given him should ease the blood flow, but he needs more specialist help. I'll arrange for an ambulance to take him." The doctor closed his medical bag and I showed him to the front door.

"Make sure he stays warm until the ambulance arrives," he advised, then climbed into his car and drove off.

More than an hour passed before the ambulance came.

"Where's the hospital?" I asked the two attendants as they lifted him on a stretcher into the vehicle.

"St Luke's in Cloverbridge," one of them replied.

I got into my car to follow them, but their vehicle was able to deal with the rough surface roads better than mine, and was soon out of sight. Fortunately, I saw some road signs to Cloverbridge and finally reached the hospital.

"You can't see your grandfather right now," a nurse told me at reception. "The doctor is examining him. It might be some time before you can visit him. Probably tomorrow." She asked if I could be contacted by phone with any news. I told her the house didn't have one.

"Then you'll have to ring us from somewhere, or come here to find out how he's getting on," she replied.

I drove back in a mood of gloomy darkness matching the night all around, worried about my grandfather, and feeling daunted at the prospect of having no other living person staying in the large house. Only perhaps, the spectral presence of that evil girl for company.

Several times in the night I woke certain I'd heard a sound. Each time cautiously opening my eyes in dread of seeing a ghost in the room. But in the low light of the lamp I saw nothing from the world beyond.

Drawing open the curtains in the morning an overcast day met me, the garden trees and bushes agitated by a strong breeze. Much as I wanted to return home, I couldn't desert my grandfather and decided that for now I'd have to remain at the house and visit him regularly in hospital. I walked into the village to ask the baker if I could use his phone to contact the hospital.

"How's he doing?" the baker saw me approaching his shop and came to the door. He was happy to let me make the call. My grandfather's condition was stable, but he remained unconscious. I said I'd drive over next day for a visit. Then I called my father to break the news.

He told me he'd also go to the hospital tomorrow, but wouldn't be able to stay locally. My mother suffered from multiple sclerosis and needed his care for most of the time. My brother Eric had stayed in the navy after the war, and was presently at sea. My father said he'd send him a telegram from the post office.

"Everyone round here wishes your grandfather well," said the baker as I was leaving. The news of his illness it seemed had already spread. Entering other stores to buy some fresh provisions, the owners' goodwill amazed and heartened me, and I was offered free of charge ham, vegetables and fruit. The old man was obviously well loved by the villagers, the generosity now handed down to me. I felt disarmingly humbled and grateful.

Back in the house the absence of my grandfather pervaded. It was if the soul had been sucked out of it. The routine of lighting fires to warm the place, keeping the kitchen range alight with coal and preparing a meal was entirely new territory to me in this property largely lost in the previous century.

After the chores I took a stroll in the garden, warily half expecting to see a ghost suddenly appearing. Thankfully none manifested, though the sense of a presence continually pervaded.

As evening approached I cooked a ham joint and boiled some vegetables, but my appetite was not up to finishing the meal, so I relaxed in the sitting room, pouring myself a generous glass or two of my grandfather's brandy on a self promise of buying a new bottle for him.

The house was eerily quiet save for the crackling of the log fire, which bestowed a feeling of warming comfort in this lonely setting. How the place must have buzzed with family life and servants back in its wealthy heyday. Now a shell of its former self.

Finishing another brandy I left for bed. In the bedroom I constantly looked over my shoulder while undressing, wondering if the girl Emily would be standing behind me. It was a relief to climb into bed, free so far of any more visitations. How long I could put up with this tense uncertainty escaped me. But for now I had a duty to remain on hand for my grandfather.

******

I WOKE, certain of hearing voices. First instinct was to bury my head under the blanket praying that if it was a haunting it would go away. But maybe someone was breaking into the house? The property being isolated, thieves might think there were rich, easy pickings.

Dressing and taking the lamp, I entered the corridor. The voices of a man and woman grew louder from downstairs. I crept to the landing and looked over the bannister to the hall below. Candles flickering in wall holders lit the setting. I'd never seen them before. The man and woman came into view heading towards the stairway. They stopped at the bottom.

"Your daughter Emily is a wicked, wilful girl. I cannot educate her any further. I would advise you to send her to a boarding school for a strong dose of discipline," the woman spoke firmly. She wore a long, grey jacket and dress, her dark hair parted neatly in the middle.

"Miss Hemming," the man replied, "I employed you as governess to educate my children Emily and Edward. I told you Emily was a difficult child. I had every confidence you would bring her to heel." Dressed in a dark suit and wing collar shirt, I realised it was the same man I'd seen on the landing the other night consoling his daughter Victoria.

These were spectres again, rising from graves of the past. My heart began racing, yet I was captivated by the events unfolding.

"Well if Emily is not packed away to an establishment that will confine her outlandish behaviour, I shall have no option other than to hand in my notice," the woman began climbing the stairway.

My fascination turned to fear as I realised the ghost was starting to approach. A dead woman whose clothes and body began disintegrating as she neared, revealing her skeleton at every upward step. I backed away, seeing her skull face seeming to stare harshly at me. Then the hall and stairway fell into darkness. Only the light of my lamp lit the landing.

The apparitions had gone, unlike my furiously beating heart. Quickly I returned to the bedroom, wishing there was a lock on the door. Not that it would keep out ghosts. But I wanted a solid shield to give me a sense of security.

How I wished for another glass of brandy from downstairs to help relieve the shock of seeing that ghoul, but dared not leave the room again that night. The supernatural gave me even greater terror than any enemy I'd encountered in war. In that, at least I stood a chance. But how could you hope to overpower ghosts? Intangibly invading your space and manipulating your mind.

So another uneasy night followed. I could only lightly sleep, if you could call it that. Waking at the slightest creak in the old property's timber joists and floorboards. The wind rattling the windows.

Though morning was a relief of sorts, from experience I knew visitations were not confined to the dark hours. I brewed myself a cup of tea in the kitchen. Then making my way across the hall to the sitting room, heard the sound of cartwheels and the trot of a horse's hooves coming to a stop on the forecourt. Opening the door, I saw a milk cart drawing up.

"Morning," a cheery man in a peak hat and striped blue and white apron greeted me, jumping down from the cart and grabbing a bottle of milk from the wagon.

"How's your grandfather doing?" he asked, handing me the bottle. The local news had obviously spread to him.

"Still in hospital. I'll be visiting him today," I replied.

The man smiled from his weathered outdoor face.

"Give him my wishes for a speedy recovery."

I nodded as he turned and climbed back on to the cart, shaking the horse's reins and setting off on his rounds again.

Soon he was gone, but the brief contact with another living person made me feel a little more at ease. And now with some fresh milk, I ate a bowl of cornflakes for breakfast before setting off for the hospital, hoping my car wouldn't shake to pieces on the potholed driveway and roads to Cloverbridge.

"Your grandfather is still unconscious," a nurse told me on arrival. "We've put him in a separate room from the main ward, so we can be sure he isn't susceptible to infections from other patients. He's in a very delicate state." The news was depressing. She led me down the corridor to the room.

"Please keep your visit brief and in no circumstances touch or breath over him," the nurse advised. "I take it you don't have a cold?"

I shook my head. We entered the room.

My grandfather looked a pathetic sight. Only his bearded, unconscious face was visible from the bedsheets. There was nothing I could do to console him. After a few minutes of watching him pityingly, I gave the bunch of grapes I'd brought to the nurse.

"Perhaps some other patients could enjoy these for now," I said. She smiled and took them.

"Ring us tomorrow, and we'll let you know if there's any improvement," she said. Making my way back down the corridor to leave, I saw my father approaching.

"Hello son," he reached out to shake my hand. "How is the old fellow?"

I told him. His expression dropped. I noticed he'd lost even more hair from his balding head since I'd last seen him and my mother only a few months ago. A few more lines under his eyes. The strain for him looking after mother in her illness was evident. I felt guilty that I wasn't being a more dutiful son, and resolved after this episode to pay more attention to them.

I waited while my father briefly visited his own father, then we found a cafe in the town to have early lunch together.

"Your grandfather and me didn't have the greatest of relationships," he confessed, his mood brought on by the fear that the old man might not have much longer in this world. I knew from some sixth sense atmosphere that existed between them, even from my boyhood, that there was a strain between them.

"I know he's always been kind to you," my father said as we sat together at a table in the cafe, "but he was quite strict to me when I was a boy. And things also soured between me and my mother." He took a bite of his ham sandwich and chewed for a moment.

"At the earliest opportunity I left home. Then not long after I married your mother," he continued.

"That house was not a happy place. Sometimes I thought I saw ghosts, but in the blink of an eye they were gone. If they were there at all that is. Strange, unpleasant events took place there."

For a moment my father's face wrinkled in a deep frown as if he was recalling a traumatic memory. I'd been wondering if I should tell him of the unearthly events I'd witnessed, but didn't want to put further weight on his mind. There was enough present worry about mother's health.

"There's a lot of guilt in that place." He took a drink of his tea.

It began to dawn on me that the heaviness of guilt hanging over the old house was now beginning to reveal its sins and secrets to me in a terrifying manner. My thought of finding different local accommodation to stay while my grandfather was in hospital was beginning to waiver. Although I didn't wish to see any more ghostly spectres, were they urging me to know their story so they could finally lay to rest in peace? And could I leave without knowing the hidden truth of events there? It was unlikely my father would tell me, even if he knew. The subject beyond enigmatic references was a no-go area with him.

"Anyway, I'd better get home to your mother," he interrupted my thoughts. "She's not too bright at the moment with her condition." We finished our lunch and left the cafe.

"I'll stay here until grandfather's well again, and let you know how he's getting on," I said as we hugged each other farewell. "Tell mum I'll be over to see her soon as I can."

I felt sad at the parting and returned to the house not in the best of moods. Unlike in London, where as well as the bombed rubble some entertainments could still be found in theatres, cinemas and nightclubs, nothing like that existed to distract the mind from worry for a couple of hours in this isolated area.

My salvation was thinking about the woman I'd set my heart on. Ruth. We'd made no firm commitment and weren't tied exclusively to each other, but I felt a bond was growing between us. Being tied to the house here, however, wasn't exactly helping to bring our relationship any closer.

I looked around downstairs to see if my grandfather had any stationery so I could write her a letter. Finally I found a door which opened into a study. Letter paper and a fountain pen rested on a mahogany bureau.

My words said nothing about the strange events I'd witnessed, but that I was holding the fort here for my grandfather and hoped soon to return so we could meet again. I sealed the envelope and left it on a small side table in the hall to post in the village next day.

Then I made sure the kitchen grate was replenished with logs so it would be hot enough to cook a meal that evening.

Thoughts of that bizarre scene I'd see in the garden a couple of nights ago came back as I stepped outside for a fresh air walk in the garden. The gazebo. That well where Emily and the boy, Edward, who I now felt certain was my grandfather in his youth, had disposed of the unfortunate fiancée Percy.

Neither well or gazebo appeared to exist in the garden now. But I decided to look around the extensive grounds just to make sure I hadn't missed seeing them.

It was hard to get precise bearings. The layout of trees and bushes in that unearthly encounter had not been foremost in my mind leading up to the poor man's murder. It took half-an-hour to make sure I'd covered every part of the grounds. Neither well or gazebo were in sight.

Walking back towards the house, a broad elm tree, which halfway up had branched into two large trunks, caught my eye. Memory flashed back. In that scene as the youngsters dragged Percy's body close to the well, there was a smaller tree nearby with a split trunk, but it would have grown considerably in over sixty years since my grandfather was a youth.

A large cluster of rhododendron bushes obscured the view of the well from the house in that earlier setting I also recalled. Now they were gone. But the elm tree remained, taller and more widespread. It gave me a bearing of where the well would once have been positioned.

I walked the twenty or so feet across the lawn to the spot. The grass layer was as flat as its surrounds. Perhaps there'd never been a well there at all, and the whole episode was a figment of my imagination. If I told anyone what I'd witnessed, they'd think I was a penny short of a pound.

Nevertheless, I was determined to investigate. There was an old garden shed at the back of the house and I made my way to it.

It was filled with gardening equipment including a petrol mower. And to one side were shovels, spades and garden forks. I selected a robust spade and returned to the spot where I calculated the well may once have existed.

Beginning to dig, at first I only uncovered soil and began thinking it was a pointless exercise. Then the spade hit something hard. A little more digging and scraping started to reveal a solid surface.

As I scraped more earth away, a large circular layer of concrete came into view. Standing back, the horrifying vision of Percy's body being tipped over into the depths of the well haunted my mind. There had been a well here, and now it became more obvious and convincing that his remains, whatever they might be now, lay in the watery depths beneath this cap of concrete.

The foot or so of soil that had hidden the covering was enough to allow grass to root and give the appearance of nothing beneath the surface. Whoever had done it, gave deliberate thought to erasing the existence of the well.

Should I inform the police about my suspicion of a body laying perhaps a hundred feet below in its depths?

"What makes you think there's a body down there?" I imagined an officer asking.

"Well, I saw this supernatural event where two youngsters disposed of a man," I heard myself replying.

The police would hardly be likely to launch a major investigation on the evidence of some oddball. I had no idea where to take it from here. The past was the past. Maybe I should just leave it there. Nothing could change it.

That evening I cut some slices from the cooked ham joint and boiled some vegetables on the range. Eating on my own in the empty house increased my sense of solitude.

In the sitting room I threw some logs on the fire and settled in an armchair with a glass of brandy and a book. The peaceful quiet began to give me the feeling that perhaps the unnatural visitations had ceased. That the house had yielded its distant past murderous secret. Then almost in the same moment of self-reassurance, I heard a woman's angry voice echoing down the hallway.

"Sit down Emily! I won't tell you again."

My heart sank. My peace shattered. Spectres were on the rise once more. What ungodly scene was now unfolding? I wanted to remain in front of the warming fire, but felt compelled to find out what was causing the commotion.

Entering the hallway with the kerosene lamp lighting the shadowy way, the sound of an argument between the woman and a young girl came from a half open door down the far end of the corridor leading towards the back of the house. I approached warily, now growing less sure of even wanting to pursue the sound. Curiosity forced me on.

I pushed the door open. The woman I'd seen on the stairs the previous night in a grey jacket and dress stood behind a desk. Emily and the boy Edward sat at two facing desks. It was a classroom. The spectres seemed unaware of my presence.

"You haven't completed your essay," the woman stormed, approaching Emily and throwing an exercise book down on her desk. "In fact you've hardly started it."

"I don't want to learn about history or arithmetic," Emily reacted scornfully. "I just want to marry someone rich and live a life of luxury, not scrape a living like you."

The girl's venom cut deeply into her governess. The woman brought her fist down on the desk, then turned and strutted out of the room, her ghostly form walking straight through me into the corridor.

The girl Emily looked towards me. She could obviously see me, but within seconds both she and Edward were gone. The room stood eerily silent and empty, only the wood panelled walls and floorboards visible in the half-light of my lamp.

I stood rooted to the spot for a few moments, nerves on edge, wondering how much more of these supernatural events I could tolerate. The memory of last night haunted me. The governess mounting the stairway, her flesh dissolving as she turned into a skeleton, her clothes shredding into fragments as she approached me. What had happened to her?

I went back to the sitting room and finished my brandy, but the relaxing atmosphere had dissolved like those spirits. I decided to go to bed. Whether I would be able to enjoy a peaceful night was becoming a gamble, but right now I had no other choice.

I threw a couple of logs on to the glowing embers of the fire I'd lit in the bedroom earlier. They crackled, sending sparks flying up into the chimney breast and shortly yielded comforting flames.

My faith in an Almighty had been tested to the point of disbelief after witnessing so many good men perishing on the wartime battlefield, but before climbing into bed that night I said a prayer in the hope of restless spirits in the house finding peace.

In the event, neither deity or spirits seemed to take any notice of it. Just as I lifted the bedding to climb in, I sensed a presence by the door. Glancing round, for a second I thought I glimpsed Emily standing there. But the image, if it had been there, was gone. I got into bed and pulled the bedclothes over my head to escape the possibility of seeing another visitation.

Unfortunately, the ghosts in this house were not so easily kept at bay.

CHAPTER 4

YET another restless sleep followed. Nerves heightened at every house creak or cry of a night animal in the surrounding countryside. But the time passed without any further unearthly incident.

Bright morning sunlight flowed into the room as I drew back the curtains, helping to lighten my mood, even beginning to delude me that perhaps now the hauntings had passed. It was enough belief at that moment to keep me going.

At the hospital I was allowed to see my grandfather for a short time. He was still unconscious and looked a pale, pathetic sight laying in the bed.

The doctor came in, a sombre looking, tall middle-aged man in a smart dark suit. He told me he believed there was a malfunction in one of my grandfather's heart valves and continued with medical jargon that meant nothing to me. But the upshot read that in his weak condition an operation to rectify it could prove fatal. The news didn't leave me feeling very hopeful for his recovery.

On the way back to the house I stopped in the village to buy some provisions, post my letter to Ruth and call my father from the baker's shop, where the owner kindly allowed me to continue using his phone. At the house I made sure fires were lit and the cooking range refuelled, then decided to read a book for a while, settling in front of the fire in the sitting room with a cup of tea.

It must have been about ten minutes later when I heard knocking on the front door. Always wondering now whether an unexpected sound heralded a new visitation, I opened the door with caution.

"Hope I'm not disturbing you," a young woman with a greeting smile and light brown hair nestling on her shoulders stood there wearing a buff trench coat.

"No, not at all," I replied, disarmed by her bright eyes and the fact she appeared to be a real being.

"I live in the house next to this one, about half-a-mile down the road. I heard that your grandfather has been taken ill," said the woman. "I've come round to pass on my good wishes for his recovery and ask if I can be of any help to you."

I was trying to work out how she could know I was the grandson. The woman read my thoughts.

"Word gets round these parts very quickly. I hope you don't think I'm intruding," her smiling expression fell, as if fearing I might have taken offence.

"No, I don't think that," I reassured her. "Come in and have a cup of tea with me."

"Only if you're sure."

"Of course, come in," I stood aside letting my visitor enter and showed her to the sitting room.

"I'm Marcia," she introduced herself as I took her coat. "And you are Tom I believe."

"News does get around here," I smiled.

"It does," she laughed.

I hung the coat on the hall stand and made the woman a cup of tea. We sat in the armchairs beside the fire.

"I understand you come from London and fought in the war," she said, holding the cup and saucer perched on the lap of her yellow dress.

"My grandfather has obviously spread the word," I replied.

"Thank God you survived that terrible business," her voice sounded heartfelt. "Unfortunately, my husband didn't make it." She lowered her head in thought for a moment.

"I'm so sorry." I felt at a loss. "What happened?"

"He was a spitfire pilot. Got shot down early on in The Battle of Britain," she paused, reflecting on the memory.

"They were bloody brave, fearless pilots," I said, deeply moved by the sacrifice those flyers had made to win the war in the air and save the country from invasion by Hitler's forces.

"I expect you saw a lot of terrible things," she looked at me.

"More than I would ever have wanted," I replied.

"Thank God it's over," Marcia took a sip of her tea. For a moment we were silent as memories filled our heads.

"Have you always lived in this area?" I asked, breaking the sadness that had briefly filled the air.

"No, I come from London too. Kensington. My late husband Richard came from these parts. He inherited the house where I live now when his father died. He was an only child and his mother had died a few years earlier." Marcia took another sip of tea.

"I met Richard when he was a young doctor working in London. I was the receptionist at the surgery. We married and moved here, where he set up his own practice. He was also a qualified pilot. He loved flying, so when war broke out he immediately enlisted in the airforce. Unfortunately he never lived to see victory." She placed the cup she held back in the saucer and put it on the side table between us.

"Anyway, enough of me. How do you find it in this old house?" she asked.

I paused for a second, wondering how to answer.

"If I'm honest. Strange."

"How so?" she gazed inquisitively.

If I told her I'd seen ghosts she might think me odd. I was enjoying her company and didn't want to drive her out believing I was missing a few marbles.

"Just atmosphere," I decided to play it down. From her continuing inquisitive look, the answer it appeared didn't satisfy her curiosity.

"I take it you know some of the villagers?"

I nodded.

"Many of them, especially the older ones, believe there were strange things going on here in the past," she said.

"Yes, I've heard," I replied, still reluctant to tell her what I'd seen.

Marcia rested back in the armchair, looking at the leaping flames in the log fire.

"I've often called in on your grandfather to make sure he's okay," she said. "He's a lovely, kind man." She paused. I felt the woman was leading to something.

"I remember, must have been a couple of years ago," she continued, "I was leaving here after visiting him to walk back to my house, when I caught a glimpse of a figure from the corner of my eye standing on the lawn. I looked round, and in a split second thought I saw a young girl in a red dress staring at me. She was gone in a flash, and for a moment I thought I'd imagined it. But to this day, I'm certain I saw a ghost." She laughed, turning to gaze at me for a reaction. "You must think me mad for saying that."

"No, I don't," I assured her. "I've seen that girl too." Her words gave me a sudden sense of relief that I wasn't losing my sanity. Someone else had also seen the spirit of my grandfather's sister.

"That means we were both imagining things, or there really is a ghost here," she said.

"Not just one, but several of them," I added. The thought of not being alone in my supernatural experience was edging me to pour out what I'd seen in a torrent.

However, the events I'd witnessed involved deeply macabre happenings related to my family, and for now I was inclined not to reveal anything intimate to a woman who appeared a friendly neighbour, but was in reality a complete stranger. The age old code of family loyalty kicked in.

I went as far as to say I believed the young girl's name was Emily, and that she'd once lived here.

"And the other ghosts...?" Marcia began, then drew back, sensing now was not the time to press any further. She smiled.

"I suppose I'd better be getting on," she stood up. "Have a few things to sort out before the day is through."

I fetched her coat and saw her to the door. Outside only my car was parked at the front so I offered to drive her back home.

"No, it's okay. My place is just half-a-mile away and I enjoy the walk. See down there," she pointed to a spot at the end of the front lawn, "there's a footpath to the side which leads back to my house." She turned to me.

"You're very welcome to visit while you're here. I'm out quite a lot during the daytime, but home most evenings, except when on night calls." She laughed seeing my puzzled face.

"No, I'm not a lady of the night. When my husband was killed in the war, I made it my mission to carry on his good works, and studied to qualify as a doctor," she explained. "It was Dr. Marsh who came out to see your grandfather when he was taken ill the other day. I work at his practice." She smiled again and made her way down the garden towards the footpath.

I stood for a while watching her depart, filled with admiration for a woman who must have been through the deepest heartbreak, but was determined not to be beaten.

******

FOR the next few nights and days I experienced peace with no ghostly visitations. Daily I visited my grandfather, who still remained unconscious, and passed the time reading books as well as taking strolls into the village to shop and chat with storekeepers, who began to see me as part of the local scene.

The evenings on my own started to feel restful, the nights undisturbed. Again I was lulled into a sense that the spirits from the other world were now at rest there. Only too soon was I proved wrong.

The following evening I'd eaten my dinner and decided to take a stroll in the garden before it grew dark. The low sun and clear sky would still provide enough light for half-an-hour or so. Walking round to the back of the house, the weather seemed to rapidly change. Clouds began to billow across the sky, and oddly the sun now appeared to be higher in the heavens as if it was earlier in the day.

A short distance away, a boy wearing a dark green gardening apron was raking up leaves on the lawn, a wheel-barrow resting near him. The rear door to the house opened and a young girl in a red dress stepped outside. Dread descended. I was experiencing another spectral visitation. The girl was Emily. The boy Edward. He stopped raking the leaves as she approached.

"When will father be back from town?" Emily asked him.

"In about an hour or so. I must get this part of the lawn cleared of leaves before he gets back, or there'll be hell to pay," the boy sounded impatient, annoyed at his sister interrupting his work.

"Make sure you've got a big pile of leaves near you to load on to the wheelbarrow," Emily ordered him. "Don't put any more in it until I get back."

Edward was about to protest, but Emily was already stepping back inside the house. The boy continued raking leaves ready to put in the barrow.

I feared the scene was leading up to another grisly event and wondered if my intervention could to stop it. I approached the boy and called to him. It was a strange sensation knowing this was my grandfather in his youth. But he continued raking, completely unaware of my existence.

The rear door of the house opened, and Emily came out followed by the governess, the woman who I'd seen dissolving into a skeleton as she climbed the stairway towards me the other night.

"What is it you want me to see?" the woman asked, continuing to follow Emily on to the lawn. She sounded terse, as if she'd been drawn away unwillingly from some other activity.

"You were telling me and Edward in the lesson the other day about different types of fungi. I think I've found one of the unusual ones growing in the lawn," Emily explained, pointing towards a spot on the turf.

The governess approached and bent down to look.

"Where?" she asked, studying the place Emily had indicated. "I can't see anything."

While the governess bent over, Emily picked up the shovel resting on the wheelbarrow and gripping the shaft with both hands raised it high, bringing the flat of the heavy metal blade with all her force down on to the woman's head. The governess' body violently jerked, then plunged forward into oblivion on the grass.

"Quick! Bring the wheelbarrow closer," Emily ordered her brother. Edward stood in a daze, shocked by his sister's wicked attack.

"You better help me, or I'll tell them you did it," the girl threatened.

The fear of serious trouble motivated him into action. He wheeled the barrow close to the senseless governess.

"Now tilt the barrow on its side," Emily barked another order. Edward obeyed.

They struggled rolling the woman's body on to the lowered edge, then lifted it upright and covered her with leaves.

The horrific scene made my blood run cold, and yet I was helpless to intervene. These were intangible moments unfolding before me. I followed as they approached the old well, which no longer existed in my modern reality, but large as life in this unholy past.

"Right, help me lift her up to the side of the well," Emily continued commanding her unwilling brother, who remained terrified of the consequences if he refused.

Again struggling with the weight of the still unconscious body, they finally managed to hoist her top half so that it slumped forward over the well wall. Emily bent down grabbing the governess' legs just above the ankles.

I thought I heard a groan from the woman, as if she was starting to regain consciousness. But to no avail. Emily forced her legs up and over, the momentum sending the body disappearing into the void, followed a few moments later by a distant splash echoing from its depths.

Edward cupped his head in his hands, as if trying to blot out the same sense of horror and shock that ran through me.

"You'd better not tell, or they'll hang you too," Emily warned her brother. Then she turned to me with a wicked smile, knowing I was standing nearby. In the next second both of them were gone.

I stood where the well once existed, but apart from the cuts in the turf I'd made earlier to reveal the concrete capping, there was no other sign of its existence. Twilight greeted me again, as the present returned. The low sun I'd left before being transported into that past nightmare had set below the horizon.

Back in the house, the restful atmosphere I'd started to enjoy in the absence of hauntings was gone. Now my nerves were on edge again at every creak of joists or distorted shadows created by lamplight. I wanted to return home, see Ruth again, get back to normality. Perhaps I could find some other local accommodation and still be able to visit my grandfather daily. My earlier resolve to remain in the house was rapidly ebbing.

Another tense night followed, no further visitations, but the images of the dreadful murders instigated by Emily cascaded through my mind.

Next morning I prepared for my hospital visit when there was a knock at the door. The postman greeted me with a smile, handing over a letter.

"How's your grandfather?" he asked. I told him he hadn't regained consciousness yet. The man frowned and expressed his wishes for a speedy recovery.

Returning to the kitchen to finish my cup of tea, I opened the letter addressed to me. It was from Ruth. My heart plunged as I read the contents. She thanked me for writing to her then began the bombshell.

"I've very much enjoyed the outings we've had together and will always cherish them, but I must tell you I'm now engaged to Simon and we plan to marry soon. He has been my close friend since childhood, and we've shared many experiences together. I've given great thought to the matter and, had both your path and mine crossed at an earlier time, things may have been very different.

"I had the feeling you may have wished for a more enduring relationship between ourselves, and it would be an unkindness allowing you to continue on a false hope. Please forgive me if this letter brings disappointment. I hope that we can remain friends, and that you will visit Simon and myself in London after we are married."

Disappointment! Her words though attempting to be kind, left me shattered. I had built so much hope on thinking we would share our lives together. Now all dashed with a few strokes of the pen.

The troubles of this house melted to insignificance. I was heartbroken and couldn't fight back the tears streaming down my face. Ruth no more. Then I felt angry at the suggestion of meeting the man she did love. The one who had stolen her from me. I had no idea how I'd fill the gap of loneliness that had opened into my soul. Somehow I would have to force myself into the routine of carrying on with what now felt like pointless everyday living.

At the hospital my grandfather remained unconscious.

"He stirs a little sometimes, but isn't really with us yet," the doctor told me. "His heart has stabilised, and we are beginning to consider the possibility that there's some other condition ailing him. We plan to carry out some further tests."

It was good news his heart condition had improved, though now replaced by a possible mystery about his health. Looking at him it was hard to imagine the elderly man laying oblivious to the world in the hospital bed had been that little boy Edward I'd seen in the visitations. And that is what puzzled me. The ghosts were of dead people, except my grandfather who was still alive. This strange business was beyond my comprehension.

CHAPTER 5

THE following two days passed without any manifestations from that world beyond the veil, and my fear of hauntings had been dulled by the heartache of losing Ruth. Sadness clouded those days and my future seemed bleak.

However, I was vividly hoisted from self-pity on the third night, while trying to bury my depression by reading a book beside the fire in the sitting room. I heard shouting. Did I want to see what was happening? To be confronted by yet more horror? Would it go away if I ignored the sound?

Curiosity once again forced me to enter the hall. They were female voices coming from behind a door along the corridor leading to the rear of the house. I approached, and with great reluctance opened it.

Inside stood Emily. Her older sister Victoria, dressed in a cream gown, was beside a treadle sewing machine holding a long piece of yellow cloth.

"How dare you accuse me of anything," Emily screamed at her.

"You were the last person to see Percy alive. You know something you're not telling me," Victoria struck back.

"Are you saying I had something to do with him disappearing?" Emily responded furiously.

I stood there knowing exactly what happened to Victoria's fiancée, but my presence didn't register.

"All I know is you're capable of being very wicked at times. I'll swear you poisoned our cat Henry because he scratched you. I saw you putting some bottle back in the medicine cupboard just after he died in agony," Victoria implied accusingly.

"I never poisoned the cat!" Emily grabbed a pair of scissors from the table beside her and flung them at her sister. Victoria flinched, just missing their impact as they hit the wall behind her.

Emily stormed out of the room, passing straight through me as if mist. The room plunged into empty darkness. The ghosts gone.

I made my way back with the lantern light to the sitting room and poured a few generous glasses of brandy, seeking solace in alcohol to wipe out an aching heart and the terror of ghouls. A temporary fix, I knew.

******

Returning from the hospital, where my grandfather remained unconscious, I stopped in the village to buy more provisions. On the way back to the car I met Marcia in the high street. She wore a smart dark jacket and skirt.

"In between house calls," she greeted me hurriedly. "Just buying a few things."

She asked after my grandfather and was about to hurry on, but paused for a moment.

"I'll be finishing duty later this afternoon. I was wondering if you would like to pop over to my house for dinner tonight?"

The prospect of spending an evening in human company, instead of spectres and lovesick depression, lifted my spirit.

"Yes, I'd be happy to," I replied.

"Good. Come over at six and you can help me out in the kitchen. Do you like fish?" she asked. I nodded.

"Right, I'll pick up some sea bass while I'm here. You can take the footpath from your garden. It's only ten minutes walk. Can't miss the house. White rendered with a red tiled roof. Must dash." She turned and strode quickly down the street, disappearing into a shop.

When I got back to the house it dawned that I'd better make myself presentable for the invite. Until now I'd dressed in casual clothes, corduroy trousers and shirts that were a little tired for smart wear. Fortunately I'd brought good white shirt, tie and dark blue suit for my stay as a just in case.

Shortly before six I made my way down the footpath from the garden, continuing across the side of a field bordered by a hedgerow. Ahead I saw the red tiled roof and white rendered house Marcia had described. The grounds of the property were spacious, though not as extensive as my grandfather's. However, the house was in far better condition than his, and the garden trees and bushes well maintained.

Marcia welcomed me at the door. She wore a knee-length maroon dress and pearl necklace in attractive contrast to the formal businesslike woman who'd earlier greeted me in the high street.

The house also contrasted with my grandfather's. For a start it had electric lighting and bright patterned wallpaper in the hallway. Marcia led me to the sitting room, furnished with a brown leather sofa and two armchairs resting on a deep pile, dark blue carpet. Framed prints of Mediterranean cafes and villages hung on the walls.

"I travelled a lot in continental Europe when I was younger. Loved those days before the war," she smiled reminiscently, noticing my interest in the prints.

"Would you like a cup of tea?" she asked. I declined, having drunk a cup not long before leaving the house.

"Right, well come with me and help prepare the meal." She led me into the hall and through a doorway into the kitchen. That too was in another universe from my grandfather's, with an electric oven, proper work surface surrounds and cupboards that didn't look as they they were on the verge of snuffing it.

Marcia gave me an apron and I took vegetable peeling duty while she gutted and prepared the sea bass. The fish was superb as we sat together eating in the dining room, once again another cared for setting, with patterned wallpaper, rich brown furniture and chairs. On a chest of drawers rested the framed photo of a good looking man with neat, side-parted black wavy hair and a chevron moustache.

"My late husband," said Marcia as I looked at the photograph.

"You must miss him very much," I remarked.

"I do," she replied. "He was a wonderful person. Time has helped me come to terms with the hurt, though I shall never forget him." She paused for a moment. "He said to me, 'if I don't come back from this war, don't let it ruin your life. Press on ol' girl.'" She smiled wistfully at the memory of his indomitable sentiment.

My parting from Ruth seemed shallow by comparison. There had been no commitment between us, just my assumption. Marcia's tragic story made me realise I had been wallowing in my trivial loss like a silly lovelorn schoolboy, and gave me a brighter, new perspective on life. I'd survived the war. I should be damn grateful for that alone.

******

AFTER the meal we relaxed on the armchairs in the sitting room with glasses of wine, facing a warming log fire.

"Are you married, or do you have someone special?" Marcia asked.

I told her briefly about Ruth, that the relationship hadn't worked out. I'd decided to put that part of my life behind me, and no longer wished to dwell on it.

"I'm sorry," she sympathised. We sipped our wine, silent for a moment.

"Have you had any more strange appearances at the house?" she broke the silence.

I wasn't sure whether to tell her about the latest apparition of the governess being murdered, but felt the need to share yet another burden weighing on me. Marcia listened to the horrifying ghostly events that had unfolded since I arrived at the house, without showing any sign of disbelief.

"You must think me mad," I said, "that I must have imagined those awful killings."

Marcia said nothing for a while before replying.

"I try to keep an open mind. There are many things we reject or disbelieve because we don't understand them. By doing that, we continue in ignorance."

I felt touched by her understanding.

"Have you considered telling the police about what you've seen?" she asked.

"I have. But I don't think they'll go to the trouble and expense of uncovering and searching an old disused well on the evidence of ghost sightings. And even if they did believe my story, any remains of bodies might implicate my grandfather as an accessory, even if it was unwilling. I could hardly be responsible for destroying his reputation and risk him spending the rest of his days in prison."

Marcia nodded, accepting my reasoning.

Our conversation moved to more of the everyday, focussing on her life as a local doctor, and my plan to resume work qualifying as a solicitor when I was able to return to London. The evening in her company seemed to end too soon.

"I'm on early call tomorrow, so I'd best be getting to bed," she said, finishing her glass of wine. "It's dark outside now, so I'll run you back in my car. Don't want you getting lost on the footpath."

I insisted I'd be perfectly okay walking. She insisted on giving me a lift.

"Won't take long in the car."

Ten minutes later Marcia drew up on the forecourt. As I opened the car door to get out, I caught sight of a light shining from a window on the second floor. I'd left no lamp lights on in the house other than one in the hall, so that I could see on my return.

"What's the matter?" she asked, noticing me staring upwards.

"There's a light coming from what I think is my grandfather's bedroom."

"He's not home yet, is he? I haven't heard that he's been released from hospital," Marcia seemed puzzled. "Are you sure you haven't left a light on in there?"

"Certain. I haven't been in the room for days," I assured her. "I'd better go and check."

"I'll come with you," she said.

"No, it's okay, I'll do it."

"No, I'll come with you," Marcia insisted for a second time that evening, opening the car door and joining me. I could hardly stop her.

Inside I picked up the lighted lantern from the side table in the hall and Marcia followed me up the stairway.

"Feels spooky," she whispered, in the shadowy surrounds.

We made our way along the landing and I cautiously opened the bedroom door, just in case there might be a human intruder. The room was pitch dark, now only illuminated by the lamp I held and showing my grandfather's unoccupied bed, a wardrobe, dresser and bedside table. There was no lamp present in the room that could have been responsible for the light.

"That's weird," Marcia sounded mystified.

I checked the other upstairs rooms with windows overlooking the forecourt, but all were largely empty of furniture, unlit and unoccupied.

"It's a very strange house," I said, "you never know what to expect next."

Satisfied there was no-one else living or risen from the dead on the landing, we made our way back downstairs to the hall. Marcia stopped at the front door.

"If it would be of help, you could stay at my house while you're waiting for your grandfather to recover," she offered. "I could make a room up for you."

"Thank you, but I think I can soldier on here." Even though it was a tempting offer to escape from the house, I didn't want to impose.

"Okay. Look after yourself. If you change your mind, let me know." She smiled and left.

A wave of loneliness descended as I closed the door. Marcia's company had lifted my spirit from the depths. Now I was down in them again. I hoped my grandfather would make a speedy recovery, not only for his own sake, but also selfishly for my own. I yearned to be back in the everyday company of people, and continue pursuing my future in the post-war new world.

That night as I lay in bed, half wondering what spectacle from the other side might suddenly present itself, my thoughts were drawn back again to the loss of Ruth. And then they strayed to Marcia. How I'd really enjoyed the evening with her. It was in that happier thought I slipped into a peaceful rest.

CHAPTER 6

FOR the first time in ages, I woke next morning feeling refreshed. The world didn't appear such a troubled place.

After breakfast I drove to the hospital. News about my grandfather's condition grew more mystifying.

"We've run tests," the doctor told me, "but we can't draw any conclusion. He's in a deep coma and how long it might last is anyone's guess. We can only wait."

That was not good news. And even less so by the doctor's continuing assessment.

"Your grandfather is in a very weak condition. It may be he never recovers from the coma. A decision by next of kin may have to be made on what steps we take next if his coma is prolonged."

The doctor was telling me in a dressed up way that in the not too distant future medical aid would have to be withdrawn, and the natural order would probably see an end to his life. That was a decision my father would have to make.

He had problems enough with my mother's poor health, so I decided to hold off a little longer from telling him the doctor's latest thoughts, hoping with a bit more time grandfather's health would improve. My sunnier start to the day had now clouded over.

Returning to the house I made a point of checking my grandfather's room, wondering if there could be some rational explanation to the light shining from the window last night. Had someone sneaked into the property, a vagrant or thief who'd escaped before Marcia and me had reached the room? With daylight shining in, it was possible I might more easily see any signs of intrusion.

Everything remained as I'd left it when making the bed and tidying the room shortly after he was taken to hospital. There was a diary on the dresser I'd noticed before, but it had a key lock. I was curious to know what might be written inside, and my temptation to open it and read the contents was only prevented by the lock.

I left the room, unable to detect any reason for the light shining from the window other than it being some supernatural manifestation.

Once again my night's sleep was uneasy, the house sounds waking me many times just as I was about to fall into a slumber. After snatches of brief rest, I noticed daylight beginning to lighten the curtains.

Glancing at my watch as I dressed, it seemed an odd new event was taking place. The watch hands pointed to just after three o'clock in the morning. The world outside should still be dark. I checked to see if the watch had stopped. It hadn't. I knew it was a reliable timepiece. There was no way I could have slept into the afternoon, and in any case the sun usually shone on this side of the house in the morning as it was now.

Opening the curtains, two figures were visible on the forecourt. Emily and Edward.

I didn't want any of this to be happening, drawn back into a paranormal time lock, but compulsive curiosity forced me on. I left the house and followed in their direction as they began walking further into the grounds. They stopped at the old well, which had once again taken form. The youngsters were in conversation beside it.

"Victoria thinks I had something to do with Percy and the governess' disappearance," Emily told her brother. "And she's accused me of poisoning Henry the cat."

"Did you poison Henry?" asked Edward. His sister ignored the question.

"I'm worried Victoria might start spreading gossip to other people. I don't want them all to start suspecting me. That would be bad for you too," she warned her brother. "Now are you sure mother and father are out, and that cook's gone to the village?"

Edward nodded.

"Then go and tell Victoria that I've found something important I'd like to show her," the girl ordered.

"What is it? I'd like to see," he said.

"You'll find out in a minute. Go and fetch Victoria."

While he was gone, Emily circled the well, her mind occupied in thought. A few minutes later Edward re-appeared coming down the garden with older sister Victoria.

"What do you want?" she asked sharply approaching Emily, a look of deep distrust in her eyes. "Is this another one of your stupid tricks?"

Emily pouted, giving the appearance of being wounded by her sister's unfriendly greeting.

"I wish you wouldn't be so harsh with me," she protested. "I really didn't have anything to do with your fiancée Percy's disappearance."

Victoria snorted contemptuously. Edward lowered his head in shame, knowing his younger sister was lying.

"What do you want?" Victoria demanded.

"I think there's a dead body at the bottom of the well," Emily announced.

"What?" Victoria's jaw dropped. She was paralysed for a moment, taking in her sister's bizarre statement.

"Now you really are making me angry. You've played some stupid tricks before, but this is outrageous." She turned to return to the house.

"No, there is a body in the well, I can see it floating," Emily called to her. "Take a look."

Her older sister turned back.

"Alright, I'll take a look. But if there isn't, I shall tell father about this and recommend he has you certified as insane."

Victoria approached the well and leaned forward over the wall to peer down.

"I can't even see the bottom. It just looks black it's so far down," her voice echoed in the void.

As her sister leaned, Emily hoisted the side of her dress and pulled out a carving knife lodged in her underwear. She raised the weapon and plunged it into the lower side of her sister's back.

Victoria jerked and groaned, slumping across the wall as blood flowed into the fabric of her light blue gown. Emily flung the knife into the well and rapidly stooped down, lifting her sister's legs and hoisting her body over the side. A distant splash rose from the depths a few moments later.

Edward stood stupefied, in a complete state of shock, then staggered throwing up on the grass. Emily smiled, satisfied with her work and rounded on her brother.

"Tell anyone, and I'll say you knew what I was planning and you helped me. They'll lock you away as well as me for the rest of your life." She walked off, leaving Edward struggling to come to terms with the violent murder of his older sister as he continued to puke on the grass.

I was in a state of shock too, witnessing the horrific scene, but felt compelled to comfort the boy. I walked towards him, when suddenly daylight disappeared. All around was silent. Only by the half light of a hazy moon could I see the surrounds. The well was gone along with the apparitions.

I made my way back to the house and poured myself a brandy in the sitting room. The embers of the earlier evening fire were still glowing and I added a couple of logs. Then sat in the armchair watching the flames growing into life as my mind grappled with the terrible murder I'd witnessed.

From an early age I had always wondered about the family whispers surrounding some unknown secrets of this house. I'd gathered that few if any of them knew exactly what had happened here. If what I was now witnessing held the truth, it was a revelation I would have been happier not to know.

Yet fate appeared to have chosen not only to expose the cursed sins of this place to me, but also to suffer the horror. It was perfectly possible for me to escape from this nightmare. I could pack my things and head home right now. Abandon the house and my grandfather. But of course, I couldn't abandon my grandfather. I could never live with myself by acting so callously.

My option was to find new accommodation nearby. The thought had now crossed my mind a number of times, but held back by the desire to keep watch over the property and make sure the house remained warm with fires, in case he quickly recovered and came home.

Now I reasoned staying somewhere else nearby would enable me to call in daily to keep the place in order. Yet strangely, something inside felt restless, unsatisfied. The story of the house was not over my senses told me. I certainly didn't want to suffer any further horror, but conversely I wanted to know the remaining secrets hovering unseen within the walls and grounds.

As I wrestled with these conflicts, seated beside the sitting room fire, sunlight began to edge through the window. My watch showed seven o'clock. This was real daylight and not a supernatural manifestation.

In the kitchen I was making a pot of tea when I heard a knock at the door.

"On my way to the surgery," Marcia greeted me at the door. "Wasn't sure if you'd be up yet. Just called to see if all is well." Her words trailed into a pause.

"You look awful if you don't mind me saying so," she appeared concerned.

I felt awful. Hair uncombed, face unwashed and covered in stubble on top of the disturbing night.

"Has something happened?" Marcia asked.

At that moment I didn't feel like telling her of the horrific spectral murder I'd witnessed.

"Would you like a cup of tea?" I asked.

"Would love a cup, but I have to get to the surgery," she apologised. "Look, why don't you stay at my house? This place doesn't seem to be doing you any good. I've got room, and I could do with a bit of company while you're here."

My wavering mind over whether I should continue in the house, or find nearby accommodation was now truly made up.

"Are you sure that would be okay? I don't want to impose."

"Of course," Marcia smiled. "I don't want to have to treat you for a breakdown in your health."

Her remark seemed to be made lightly, but nearer to the truth than she may have realised.

“Pack your things and bring them over at one o’clock. I’ve some house calls to make in the village, but I’ll pop over at lunchtime. You can park on the forecourt.” She said goodbye and returned to her car.

The prospect of leaving the house, but being nearby to keep an eye on the place lifted a great weight off my mind. Though even as I left, the grip of Emily on my life somehow seemed to follow me.

As I arrived at Marcia's house, she pulled up behind me on the forecourt. After I'd unpacked, we sat in the kitchen with a cup of tea and eating cheese and tomato sandwiches she'd made.

"You could do with a good rest," she said as we finished lunch. "Go and have a lie down in the bedroom. I'm sorry it's a bit sparse, but it hasn't been occupied for some time. Must hurry now for my next house call."

The sparse bedroom, as she'd described it, was luxurious compared to the one at my grandfather's. For a start it had a carpet. The room was similarly panelled, though somehow the dark wood seemed to shine with a cared for lustre. The bed linen looked fresh and inviting and the greatest plus was having an electric light, without the pungent vapour that poured from kerosene lamps.

Before taking a rest, I had the further luxury of a nearby bathroom with hot bathwater supplied from an electric geyser. Then to bed, where I sank into a deep, refreshing sleep.

A knock at the door woke me.

"I'm making dinner," Marcia called. "Ready in half-an-hour." I looked at my watch. It was nearly seven in the evening.

"I managed to get these sausages from the butcher," she told me as we sat to eat in the dining room. "Still rationing shortages from the war, and they aren't always available here."

"I must pay you for the accommodation and food," I said.

"Just make a contribution for the food. I'm not short of money," she replied.

"Pays well as a doctor," I remarked, then realised that may have sounded rude.

"Not for the hours of work I put in," she said, taking no offence. "The parents of my late husband, Richard, owned an engineering company," Marcia explained. "It was very successful and Richard owned shares in it as a sleeping partner. When he died, the shares transferred to me. I didn't want to be part of the enterprise, not my province, so I sold the shares and invested the money. I hardly touch it, but occasionally it helps with an extra expense to be covered. I lead a fairly frugal life."

"With all your work you manage to keep this place in an amazingly good condition," I said. She laughed at my remark.

"I'm no wonder woman. Mrs Ballantyne, a lovely lady who lives in the village comes to clean it once a week. I couldn't keep it clean like this on top of my long work hours."

After helping Marcia with the washing up, we settled in the sitting room with a pot of tea in front of the cosy fire. A sense of happiness that I hadn't felt in a long time began to settle over me.

"I have one of my rare days off tomorrow," she said as we drank tea, "I was wondering if you'd like to go out with me in the car? Take in some of the local area. Have a look in Beresford, our nearby town."

"I'd love to," the invite was an unexpected pleasant surprise. As we chatted, the phone in the hall began ringing.

"Just a moment," Marcia got up from the armchair and left to answer it. A few minutes later she returned.

"I'm sorry, but I have to go out. Someone in the village has been taken ill and I'm still on duty until tomorrow. May not be back until late," she explained. "Don't stay up." She hurried out.

I was annoyed at a truly relaxing evening being brought to an abrupt end. Then I reprimanded myself for being selfish. Some poor soul was unwell. Marcia had to rush out to them, and here I was still sitting comfortably in front of a warm fire. By eleven o'clock she still hadn't returned. I went to bed feeling even greater admiration for the woman's self-sacrificing work.

******

WHEN I woke again, Marcia was calling me from outside the bedroom.

"I'm making breakfast. Don't be long."

Downstairs in the kitchen she served bacon with fried eggs and toast. Delicious.

"I got back at about three this morning," she told me. "The young son of a local farmer fell from a barn loft where he'd been helping his father stack hay. Broke his right arm and leg. I had to straighten the bone fractures so they wouldn't start trying to heal out of place," Marcia shook her head.

"Poor boy was screaming in agony. I gave him a shot of morphine and waited until the ambulance arrived. Took hours because the vehicle broke down on the way there."

"You must be exhausted," I said, "we can put off going out."

"No, I get used to catching short snatches of sleep in this line, and I've been looking forward to a day out for a couple of weeks now. A locum's covering for me today."

Before our outing, Marcia drove me to the hospital where my grandfather remained unconscious, with no change reported in his condition. Hopefully, tomorrow he might show some sign of progress was the only news the doctor could offer.

While travelling with Marcia, thoughts of Ruth crept into my mind, and the deep hurt I'd felt by being rejected. But now the episode didn't seem so painful with Marcia beside me.

Perhaps the fates had guided, and Ruth was never destined for me. It was not the first time in my life that some unpredictable event had pushed me in another direction. The war for one. I could only hope whatever shift was now taking place, this time would be for the better.

I was beginning to feel a fondness for Marcia, but dare not run away with any idea that my destiny lay in that direction. She was just helping a stranger who was many miles from his home.

We visited the market square in Beresford town, looking round the traders' stalls crowded with eager buyers including Marcia, buying a brown leather handbag and a necklace. Then we found a cafe and had lunch. Her tired look in the morning had now been replaced by rosier cheeks, which pleased me.

I linked my arm in hers as we walked along the high street, for a second wondering if such a friendly gesture might be an intrusion too far. She looked at me and smiled, sending a warm glow through me.

On the way back we took a detour, stopping for a countryside walk and later enjoying tea and cakes in the village cafe. That evening I made the dinner and we settled for a while with glasses of sherry in the sitting room. All to soon my happy day was over.

"Hope you don't mind, but I've a really early start tomorrow and I'd better get some sleep," said Marcia, finishing her drink and preparing to leave the room.

I wanted to kiss her goodnight to show how much I'd enjoyed her company. A desire that for now though, would probably be a step too far. We'd had a good day together. I didn't want to risk spoiling it.

CHAPTER 7

MARCIA had left the house when I woke next morning. I made breakfast, then while clearing up heard the clatter of a horse and cart approaching on the paved forecourt.

From the kitchen window I saw the same milkman who made deliveries to my grandfather's house. He reined in the horse bringing the cart to a halt and jumped down. He gave a surprised look seeing me opening the front door as he approached.

"Just lodging temporarily," I said.

"None of my business," he replied, giving me a knowing wink and thrusting a bottle of milk into my hand. I closed the door hoping he wasn't going to set up chain of salacious gossip about the newcomer and the village doctor.

At the hospital I received some hopeful news, followed by a shock.

"Your grandfather stirred a little last night," the nurse informed me. "He mumbled something under his breath about someone falling into an old well in a garden. Do you know who or what he might have been talking about?"

I shook my head. I didn't want to tell her what I'd seen. The possibility my grandfather could be implicated in gruesome murders.

"Are you alright?" she asked.

I must have suddenly looked pale. Whatever coma he was in, something about the past was obviously stirring in his mind. I had only seen ghosts of the past and had no tangible evidence of crime being committed. The nurse's words virtually confirmed to me that my grandfather knew an old well had once existed in the garden, and that a body or bodies really did lay hidden down there.

Satisfied I wasn't unwell, the nurse looked at a form on the clipboard she held.

"From tests, the doctor says there's nothing he can diagnose as to why he remains in this condition, but it's good that he appears to have shown a slight sign of consciousness. We'll keep you informed of any further developments." The nurse smiled and left the room.

"See you tomorrow," I whispered to my grandfather, hoping this possible improvement might enable him to at least hear me. There was no response. Now my concern was that he might give some confession to his part in the horrifying killings while still unconscious.

That afternoon, with a feeling of great reluctance, I took the footpath from Marcia's house to my grandfather's in order to check all was well. The fires had gone out and I spent some time relighting them, just in case he made a speedy recovery and came home.

As I left the sitting room and began crossing the hall to leave, I caught sight of two figures standing at the bottom of the stairway. A middle-aged, grey haired man wearing a dark suit and white wing collar shirt. A woman dressed in a turquoise, bell-shaped gown hugging her tightly at the waist. Light brown ringlets spilled over on each side of her centre parted hair. She appeared several years younger than the man.

I recognised him as the same spectre I'd seen on the landing that night when I first arrived, doing his best to comfort Victoria over missing fiancée Percy. My heart sank. I'd been in the house for about an hour and was already being haunted again. The spectral woman with him sounded angry and upset.

"We've now had two governesses since the first one disappeared without trace," she said. "Both have resigned saying Emily is wilful and refuses to behave or learn. And she threw a china ornament at me today when I asked her to tidy her bedroom."

It began to dawn on me this was Emily's mother.

"I know she can be difficult, Vera, but it's probably her age. I'm sure she'll grow out of it," father defended.

"I'm sorry to say it about our own daughter, but I think the girl is wicked." the woman ignored his attempt at defence. "Now that Edward is away at naval college, I'm of a mind that we should send Emily to a finishing school. Preferably a long way from here, because I'm at my wit's end with her."

"I'll consider what to do," the man replied. They started walking towards the front door. It was closed, but held no barrier to these apparitions as they disappeared through the solid wood.

Only for my grandfather's sake did I feel duty bound to watch over the place. God knows, I never wanted to step inside the house or its grounds ever again if I could be free of that duty. And even now the visitations were not yet over.

A girl appeared from an open doorway opposite me in the hall. I didn't recognise her for a moment. Then I realised it was Emily, though no longer the youngster I'd last seen. Her face fuller, moving into early womanhood, her figure more developed, wearing a long, dark blue gored skirt and puffy-sleeved, cream lace blouse. Her increasing beauty belied the evil that dwelt within.

While the other spectres had been unaware of my presence, Emily saw and sensed me perfectly. She gave me a cunning grin.

"You heard my mother," she said. "Don't you think it's unkind that she wants to send me away?" Emily wasn't waiting for a reply. She began walking towards me as if living flesh and blood. My own blood running cold. Her eyes glistened with malice.

"Now you see why I shall have to do something about her. I can't have my mother wanting to send me away." Almost reaching close enough to touch me, her image dissolved. I stood in the hallway alone, my mind reeling yet again from another bizarre encounter with the dead.

I made a swift exit from the place, returning to Marcia's house with the vision of the ghosts weighing heavily, especially the malicious look in Emily's eyes. Time had obviously passed in the narrative of that spirit world, and although she was now on the cusp of adulthood, Emily's evil mind apparently remained.

Yet something more terrifying began to crystallise in my thoughts. I recalled grandfather telling me that while he was a young man away at naval college, he was summoned home on news his mother had suddenly disappeared. A heartbreaking event coupled with financial problems that ended with his father dying a year later.

Had Emily murdered her own mother too?

I'd been subjected to enough traumatic supernatural revelations, I didn't want to suffer any more. I couldn't just abandon caring for my grandfather's house, but until he was ready to return home I couldn't tolerate visiting the place any longer. Whatever other secrets the place held, they were in the past, and I only wanted to continue moving into the future. Yet I sensed the house and Emily had not finished with me yet.

Marcia returned at eight that evening. She looked pale and exhausted.

"What a day," she said as I brought her a cup of tea in the sitting room while she relaxed in front of the fire. "Morning surgery was packed, and then I had more than the usual number of house calls to make. People seem to be going down with illness like ninepins. Some nasty infections around at the minute."

"Well I hope you don't catch any of them," I sat down in the armchair beside her.

"Hazard of the job," she laughed. It was wonderful enjoying her company again as we chatted for a while, helping to push the bizarre events of the afternoon into a distant compartment of my mind for now.

"Right, better get something to eat," she said, finishing her tea and beginning to stand up.

"No, I'll do it," I raised my hand signalling her to remain seated. "I bought a couple of beefsteaks in the village after leaving grandfather's house. Thought I'd get us a treat. Seems the food rationing is easing a little."

"I like chocolate even more," she said.

"Hasn't eased that much," I replied with a smile, and left for the kitchen.

******

"How was your day?" Marcia asked, as we sat together eating in the dining room. She immediately detected a change of mood in my face, the memory of the haunting beginning to cloud the happy moment I was sharing with her.

"Did I say something wrong?" she appeared concerned and stopped eating.

"It's okay, don't worry." I didn't want her upset, but she persisted.

"Come on. What's happened?"

I told her of the ghosts I'd seen. My fear that Emily was planning another murder. Marcia said nothing for while, considering what I'd told her.

"But from what you say, these ghosts are in the long past. Whatever the truth of it, there's nothing you can do to change it," Marcia attempted to reassure me.

"I know I can't change the past, but that's the point," I explained. "It's knowing I'm utterly powerless to change it. A cold-blooded, psychopathic murderer of anyone she dislikes or who opposes her. And the way she tricked my grandfather into being an accomplice. It shatters me to the soul."

Marcia reached out and placed her hand on mine. A soft, comforting touch. For a second our eyes met, forming an unspoken bond between us.

"If it's so troubling to you, I can visit your grandfather's house to make sure everything's okay there," she offered.

"No, you've enough to do, I couldn't put that on you for a minute," I declined the kind offer. "He's showed some signs of recovering, and I'd hate him to come home to a cold house with no provisions. I'll carry on doing it."

"You're worrying too much," said Marcia. "If your grandfather does come out of his coma, they aren't going to send him home immediately. They'll want to make sure he's fully recovered first. You'll have time to prepare."

"Your the doctor. I'm sure you know best," I smiled.

After eating the meal we settled together by the fire in the sitting room. But however comforting Marcia's words, I couldn't lose the nagging feeling that even now Emily was watching and waiting for me, knowing I'd be returning to the house.

******

OVER the next few days I passed the time visiting my grandfather, and driving one afternoon to Beresford town where I'd spent the day with Marcia. It wasn't as enjoyable without her, but I liked the bustle of street life in contrast to the quieter village surrounds where I was staying.

Returning on the third day from the hospital, I saw a grey-haired woman in a blue apron coming out of the dining room holding a feather duster. She looked to be in her mid-fifties. The lady stared at me in surprise. I was equally surprised to see her.

Then we both broke into laughter as I remembered Marcia had a weekly cleaner, and the woman realised who I was.

"You must be Mr Roberts," she said. "The doctor told me you were staying here for a while." The woman approached me. "Your poor granddad's in hospital, isn't he? Lovely man. I'm so sorry to hear he's been taken poorly." She seemed genuinely sorrowful.

"That house he lives in is just too much for him to look after at his age. I've offered to clean round it for a reduced rate, but he won't have it. Obstinately independent, and now look where it's got him," she frowned. "Carries a lot of mysteries that place. Strange things happened there in the past, so people say."

She stopped, suddenly realising she might be talking out of turn to a relative of the family.

"Of course, it's all just old village gossip, I'm sure," she attempted to play it down. I could have assured her from what I'd experienced that the village gossip was not far off track. But I had no reason to tell her, since my story of ghosts would only fuel more gossip, and I was hardly likely to implicate my grandfather as an accessory to murder.

"Anyway, better get on with cleaning," she said, adding with a wry grin, "the doctor is lucky to have a handsome chap like you staying here for a while."

I guessed another rumour mill was being built in the village about the lady doctor and her new male lodger. Crafty nods and winks all round, no doubt.

Truth is, I wished the rumours could be right. I found myself more and more attracted to Marcia. Except the gossip likely had more going for it than the reality. I hoped there was some kind of affinity between us, but I didn't want to set myself up for another let down. Marcia had shown nothing other than friendship.

The sound of a vacuum cleaner bursting into life from the sitting room shook me out of any further romantic wishes, prompting me to move on with the rest of the day.

CHAPTER 8

AFTER walking to the village to buy fresh food, I took a stroll in the large garden surrounding Marcia's house, enjoying the warm afternoon sunlight.

It must have been ten minutes or so of relaxing when I glanced across at a broad oak tree that I guessed must have been there for at least a couple of hundred years. My heart suddenly skipped a beat. I could swear I saw Emily standing in the shadow of the trunk. In a second the image was gone.

I continued my stroll feeling considerably unsettled, fearing the place I thought was a refuge from hauntings was not immune to her following me. But after a while I dismissed the vision as a hangover from the horrors I'd experienced. Just a fleeting blip of imagination surfacing from a burdened brain.

When Marcia returned in the evening, once again I prepared a meal for us then we settled with a glass of wine by the fireside.

"I suppose you'll be going back to your law work in London," she said, after telling me a little of her day.

"That's the idea," I replied. "Beginning to feel at a loose end here. I had hoped for it to be a relaxing break, but things have worked out rather differently."

"Yes, traumatic to say the least," she sympathised.

We sat silently for a while, just enjoying our company and the warmth of the fire.

"I suppose you'd never consider finding work with one of our law firms in town and living somewhere in the area?" Marcia broke the silence. I was surprised by the question.

"It isn't a thought that's ever entered my head," I replied. "Apart from overseas service, London's the only place I've ever known. Why do you ask?"

"Oh, nothing in particular. Just that I know a local solicitor with a practice in Beresford who's looking for another partner in the business," she said. "You told me you were qualifying in company law, and that's the field of experience he's looking for."

"Yes, but I've still got the final exam to do. The war put a temporary kibosh on that," I explained.

"Well the opportunity will still be there in three months or so, which would give you time to get things in place. He's just putting out feelers now." Marcia took a sip of wine. "Only thought I'd mention it. But for a city boy like you it would probably be too far from life in the metropolis."

I didn't know what to say other thanks for letting me know. Was this purely a kind offer of putting a job opportunity my way, or was she suggesting it for some other reason? The thought of remaining near Marcia was tempting. But I still didn't want to start running away with ideas that could just be a figment of my imagination.

That night I lay in bed thinking over what Marcia had said. Maybe I should look for a new way of life. Perhaps I was being narrow minded always thinking London was the only place to live. I'd been fortunate to survive the war, now perhaps I should reconsider my future direction. Take chances on a new horizon.

Marcia called me next morning with the invitation to scrambled egg and toast for breakfast.

"Must get going," she said, after we'd eaten. "Lots of house calls today."

"Would be good if we could spend another day out together," I suggested.

"Sunday. I've got that off. A few more days and we'll have another outing. See you this evening." She left for work.

I hadn't checked my grandfather's house for several days, and was beginning to feel guilty about neglecting the property. After my daily visit to him in hospital, I resolved to call in at the house and make sure everything was okay. It was a decision I came to regret.

******

THE atmosphere inside the property felt dank and foreboding. The fires had gone out and the lack of warmth in the stone building made me shiver. My footsteps in the hall echoed up the empty stairway and along the corridors.

Cautiously I looked into the rooms half expecting to be confronted by a spectre. With every step I sensed the presence of Emily following me. Several times I felt my skin creep and looked behind wondering if she was there, but her spirit stalked me unseen.

After checking over the property, with great relief I left to make my way back to the welcoming atmosphere of Marcia's house. Nearing the footpath that led to her home, I felt drawn to taking a look at the spot where the old well had once stood.

The capping I'd uncovered by digging out the turf was still visible. It troubled me the bodies, or at least the bones of the innocents that Emily had dispatched into the depths, still lay there. They should at least be retrieved for a decent burial.

I turned to resume my way back to the footpath when I heard two women's voices. Looking behind, Emily and her mother were strolling in the grounds close by. The old well wall had suddenly become intact. In that brief second I'd been plunged into the spirit world again.

"I'm so sorry for behaving badly towards you," said the adolescent Emily, dressed in a blue gown.

"My dear, I'm glad you've realised the error of your ways," her mother replied, appearing commandingly stern in a long grey dress. "The finishing school in Suffolk that your father and I are sending you to, will help develop skills of etiquette and refinement. I'm sure that will serve to attract a young gentleman of good means to support you in marriage."

"I'm so pleased you've forgiven me," Emily spoke humbly. It seemed an amazingly changed Emily to the one I'd encountered previously. Perhaps her reign of horror was over.

"Your father will be back from his business meetings in the city in a couple of days, and will be here to wish you goodbye," her mother continued.

"God! The cat's just fallen into the well," Emily grabbed the woman's shoulder.

"Violet?"

"Yes, she jumped on to the wall and must have lost her balance," Emily lied, rushing towards the well. Her mother quickly followed, leaning over the wall to look into the depths.

"We must fetch help," she cried. "I can't see anything in that darkness."

Even as the words were leaving her mother's mouth, Emily had stooped down behind pulling at her ankles and pivoting her body over the wall.

"What are you doing?" the woman shrieked. "Let go!"

But Emily didn't let go. Her mother's hands had a shaky grip on the rim of the well and she was desperately struggling to keep hold. To no effect, as Emily forced her outstretched legs further upwards until the woman could grip the edge no more. In another second her hold was broken and she plunged into the void, a scream cut short as she impacted on the water below with a reverberating splash. Deathly silence followed.

It happened so quickly, that even if I'd had the power to intervene, I could not have raced the twenty feet in time to stop it.

Emily looked across at me and smiled that evil, proud smile of satisfaction in her work. Then she was gone. The spirit world enclosing me evaporated.

No matter the several times I'd witnessed her acts of merciless killing, each successive one left me more and more stunned. And now she had murdered her own mother.

When Marcia returned that evening, she remarked on how pale and drawn I looked. I cooked some food for dinner, but had no appetite to eat it. As we settled together in the sitting room, the silence between us was interrupted only by the crackle of the log fire.

"What's happened?" Marcia asked. "You look so troubled."

I didn't want to burden her with my thoughts, she had enough responsibilities caring for the sick. But being plagued by paranormal horrors virtually every time I visited my grandfather's house was now seriously fraying my nerves. I relented and told her what I'd witnessed that day.

"Do you think I'm just imagining it? Do you think I'm insane?" I asked, beginning to doubt my own sanity.

"As a doctor, I've been called on several times to certify people as insane," she said, looking across at me from her armchair. "I don't consider you on that scale. And if I did, there is no way I'd have invited you to stay here."

Her verdict heartened me.

"As I told you, once I thought I caught a brief glimpse of that girl fitting your description of Emily on your grandfather's lawn. Now either we are both mad, or the possibility of her spirit exists. It seems you have greater confirmation of that than me."

We talked a little longer, mostly about where we would go for an outing on Sunday when she had time off. It helped take my mind away from that terrible murder. I was grateful for Marcia's company. Maybe it was her professional doctor's manner. I hoped it was much more than just that.

Later that evening, making our way to bed, we said goodnight to each other on the landing. I wanted to hold and kiss her. In her eyes I thought I sensed the same feeling too. But if I was misreading her feelings, such a move would result in embarrassment for both of us and spoil the friendship. We parted for our rooms.

In bed I lay awake thinking about Marcia. The thought of leaving her behind when I finally returned to London was becoming increasingly difficult. Then Ruth came into my mind. Although I had been certain she was the woman I wanted to marry and spend my life with, it all seemed curiously different now. Clearer that her 'Dear John' letter had hurt my pride more than any deep feelings I held for her. I'd been in love with love. Someone to cling to after the desperate days of wartime. We'd never pledged any strong feelings between us. Then on the other hand, neither had Marcia and me. But at least I'd formed a bond with her during my stay here. A closeness that hadn't existed with Ruth.

In this balancing act between heart and logic, I gradually fell asleep, troubled now by dreams of Emily's cold-blooded disposal of her mother in the old well. The uneasy night's sleep was shortened by a knock on the bedroom door at six in the morning.

"The hospital's phoned," Marcia called. "Your grandfather has regained consciousness and he's asking for you."

I was thrilled by the news and quickly dressed to leave. Little did I know at that moment, the horrors of the past had still not been laid entirely to rest.

******

"YOUR grandfather is still in fragile health, so I don't want you to stay too long," the senior ward nurse told me, as she opened the door to let me into his room.

Wearing a light blue pyjama top, he was sitting up in bed resting his back on a couple of pillows.

"I'm so glad you're awake again," I greeted him. He raised a weak smile on his pale face, the effort of forming a curve in his lips almost a struggle.

"And I'm glad to see you again, my boy," he replied in a soft, slightly faltering voice. I bent over and gently hugged his shoulders. He pointed to a chair beside a radiator in the room.

"Pull that up."

I drew it close and sat down beside him.

"I've been a lot of trouble to you, haven't I?" he looked at me apologetically. "The nurse tells me you've been visiting daily for some time. I'm sorry if I've upset your plans."

"My only concern has been for you," I assured him. He raised another weak smile in appreciation.

"I don't think it's been your only concern though," he said, after a short pause. He could see from my expression that I was puzzled by what he meant.

"I think you know more about past events at my house than you did before you arrived." He stared at me, his eyes reading the knowledge reflected in mine. "About Emily. About me. The horrific murders she carried out, and how I helped her." His look grew distant for a moment, steeped in memory.

"How do you know that?" I was mystified.

"Pour me some water," he said, raising his arm with strained effort and pointing to a jug and glass on his bedside table. After taking a drink he settled back on the pillows.

"While I've been unconscious, I believe I've been on what some would call an astral plane, triggered that evening not long after you first arrived. You went to relax in the lounge while I was preparing the evening meal. A short time later a strange feeling came over me. As if I was being drawn back into the past."

It jogged my memory of when I'd gone to the lounge to read a book, and was confronted by the ghost of Emily. She asked me to follow her and I witnessed her first murder, the poisoning of Victoria's fiancée, Percy. When I returned to the house, I found my grandfather unconscious on the kitchen floor.

"I came over dizzy and only returned to my senses in the early hours of this morning," he continued. "But from time to time while I was unconscious, somehow my inner spirit returned to those horrific events of the past on some parallel supernatural plane, and I sensed you were there witnessing them, and learning that your grandfather as a boy helped Emily to carry them out. God, the guilt I've carried all my life helping her in those dreadful murders."

I saw teardrops forming in his eyes.

"It's okay. I don't hold anything against you." It worried me the trauma would cause him to collapse again. "I know that Emily threatened you. Terrified you into thinking you would hang or spend the rest of your life in prison," I assured him. He stared searchingly at me.

"How can you ever forgive what I've done?"

"I know you were forced into it," I tried to reassure him again. He looked so pale I feared he would suffer another seizure. "You should get some rest now. I'll come back tomorrow when you're feeling better."

"No," he raised his arm limply, gesturing for me to stay. "There is more to tell. Something you didn't witness in that parallel dimension."

I'd stood up to leave, but he was determined for me to remain. I sat again, waiting while he wiped a trickle of teardrop from his cheek.

"I told you that after my father died I became the owner of two shop businesses in the village, and that I'd met the woman, Mary, who would become your grandmother."

I nodded, recalling his story.

"At the time, Emily was still living at the house. She was no longer a child by then and hated the prospect of me marrying. She'd always been dominating, and took strongly against the possibility of this new woman having greater influence over me." He paused and pointed to the water jug. I poured another drink.

"I was worried," he continued. "I knew what that evil sister of mine was capable of, and feared my new wife, Mary, would end up dead at the bottom of the old well. It had always troubled me how our mother had suddenly disappeared while I was away at naval college, and one day I confronted Emily about it." He shook his head in agitation recalling the occasion.

"At first she stared at me angrily, as if I was accusing her of doing something terrible. But she knew I knew what she was capable of doing. Her angry stare turned into an evil smile. She said 'that's what happens to people I don't like'. At that moment I realised my poor mother also lay at the bottom of the well, as I'd suspected." He shook his head again. "Of course she started the usual threats of if you tell on me, they'll hang you too."

I told my grandfather that I'd seen the terrible murder of his mother on that parallel supernatural plane as he'd described it.

"But the events didn't end there," he said. "That time when you'd first arrived, I wasn't exactly truthful when I told you Emily left the house one day and never returned."

His eyes clouded into distant memory again.

"A few days before I was due to marry Mary, I was in the garden trimming back some shrubs, when Emily came up to me. She asked, 'are you certain about getting married?' I told her I loved Mary and it was my dearest wish. Her expression turned grim."

My grandfather reached out for the glass of water I now held for him, his own grip too weak to grasp it for long. He took another sip, pausing again before continuing.

"She said to me, 'if Mary comes here to live, I will make life hell, and won't be held accountable for what else I might do'. I knew exactly what she meant about not being accountable, and that Mary's life would be in mortal danger. Emily then walked off towards the gazebo, confident I think that her threat would make me change my plans and that I'd call off the wedding. I was furious."

Now my grandfather paused for breath, the memory of harrowing events was rapidly tiring him. I told him to rest, but he insisted on continuing.

"I went back inside the house and to a cupboard where my father had kept his old hunting guns. I chose one and loaded it with a cartridge," he paused for more breath. "I went back into the garden and walked across to the gazebo where Emily sat enjoying the warm summer sunshine. She saw me carrying the gun and stood up, starting to laugh. 'You're not going to shoot me, are you? You're too weak to have the courage,' she goaded me. I knew that as long as Emily remained here, my life would always be unhappy. She was domineering, unhinged, without any feeling for others. She would murder Mary, I had no doubt."

He reached out to me for another drink of water. He could see I was about to advise him to rest, but shook his head insisting on continuing.

"I raised the gun and aimed the barrel at her. She laughed again. I said if you even harm a hair on Mary's head, I will kill you. She laughed even more, calling me pathetic, that I didn't have the courage to shoot a rabbit. My mind blanked out for a moment. I was only aware of a loud blast. Then in front of me red started colouring the chest of Emily's yellow dress, surrounding a large hole blown into it. She was falling backwards, a look of amazed horror on her face." He lowered his head for a moment.

"Strangely, I should have felt terrible, but a wave of unbelievable relief coursed through me. An evil that had polluted all of my life was gone. I stood over her, relishing that surprised look etched in her face as she lay there stone dead."

My grandfather looked at me, I think expecting I should be shocked. It was another shocking revelation, but I understood why he would have been driven to that extreme.

"In a final irony," he said, "I disposed of her body down the old well, then not long after demolished the wall and capped that awful abyss, saying a prayer for the innocents, but hoping Emily would descend into the depths of hell."

He grew more breathless, struggling to continue. I strongly insisted he should rest. Again he asked me to stay.

"The secret of what you did will remain only with me," I promised him, worried that he thought I would expose his confession.

"No, I want it to be known by the authorities," he said. "I'm probably not long for this world. I don't wish to go to my maker unforgiven for not confessing my sins. And it is the only way of laying the curse of my sister to rest. To exorcise the evil that hangs over the house."

"I don't think the police would believe what happened there all those years ago just on your word or mine," I told him.

"I've written everything down in a dated locked diary that I keep in my bedroom," he replied.

I remembered seeing the diary, wondering what was inside.

"The key is kept in the bottom drawer of my dresser, underneath some papers. Give it to the police."

He was putting me in an impossible position. The revelation wasn't going to bring back the dead. It could only result in my grandfather spending the remaining days of his life in prison after he recovered. He saw the dilemma in my eyes.

"Please do this for me," he pleaded. I nodded agreement, but still felt unsure of carrying out his wish. I was about to insist again that he must rest, when the nurse entered and saw him.

"You've exhausted the poor man," she harangued me," how's he going to get better? Come on, say goodbye and go." She stared sternly at me to make sure her order was obeyed.

"See you tomorrow," I said, lightly clasping his shoulders.

"So glad you came to stay with me," he raised a smile. "I'm sorry to have caused you so much trouble."

I was about to reassure him there was no need to apologise, but the nurse hurried me out.

CHAPTER 9

I RETURNED to my grandfather's house and warily entered the property, fearful of yet another haunting. Retrieving the diary and key from his bedroom, I quickly made my way back to the front door.

For a moment in the hallway, I was sure I heard a female voice calling my name. Looking behind there seemed to be a figure standing in the corridor leading to the rear garden. Within a split second it disappeared. A shiver ran through me as I left.

Back at Marcia's I settled in the sitting room and read through my grandfather's diary. It recorded all those harrowing murders he'd been forced into as Emily's accomplice, reaching back into his boyhood.

I strained to hold in tears, feeling the guilt and fear he had suffered, laid bare in the intimate emotions of his written words. How he carried that weight for so long without losing his sanity was beyond me. When Marcia returned that evening, she gazed at me in deep concern.

"What's the matter? You look totally drained. Has something happened to your grandfather? Have you seen another ghost?"

I assured her my grandfather was slowly recovering and that I hadn't suffered another haunting.

"It's been a difficult day," I said. "Can we talk another time?" I declined her offer of food. "Just want an early night." She respected my wish.

The prospect of an early night's rest was a vain hope. I wrestled over my grandfather's desire to hand his diary over to the police. I could never forgive myself if he spent the rest of his days in prison.

Lapsing eventually into a light sleep, I dreamt of being in the garden with him. We walked together in warm sunshine. He stopped and turned to me.

"The curse of my sister Emily no longer survives. It has now passed with my own ending. I wish you a happy life." He smiled at me then began walking away, disappearing in the air.

The phone ringing downstairs in the hall woke me. It was four thirty in the morning. The ringing stopped. I could hear Marcia speaking and presumed it was someone seeking her medical advice. A short time later there was a knock at my bedroom door.

"The hospital is calling," she said. "They want to speak to you."

Quickly I put on shirt and trousers and went to the phone.

"Mr Roberts?"

"Yes."

"I'm staff nurse Helen Maguire. I'm very sorry to tell you, but your grandfather passed away half-an-hour ago."

I was totally stunned. The news took me by complete surprise. I knew he still had some way to go to full recovery, but I truly thought he was on the mend. My dream of walking with him in the garden just before the phone call. Had he visited me to bid farewell?

"Hello, are you still there?" asked the nurse.

"Yes," I replied. "I'll come in to collect his belongings and make arrangements."

Marcia could tell the news was not good.

"I'm so sorry," she put her arm around my shoulders. We went into the kitchen and she made a cup of tea. I told her about my grandfather's deathbed confession and of his diary.

"I can't imagine anyone could condemn him knowing the full story," she sympathised.

"Yes, but people can be unkind. I'm reluctant to tell the police, to hand over his diary, even though that was his wish. He was well liked. I don't want to taint his good name."

I looked at Marcia for some type of guidance as we sat at the kitchen table.

"That's a family matter for you to decide," she said. "If I told you what I thought, and you later regretted following my advice, I would hate it to cause a rift between us."

She was right, it was a burden for my shoulders.

******

AFTER making arrangements for my grandfather to be interred at the local church in a couple of weeks time, I thanked Marcia for her kindness and hospitality before going home to my apartment in London. I promised to keep in touch by phone until I returned for the funeral.

Back home it was refreshing to be surrounded by the business of city life again, though the rubble of bombed streets still littered much of the landscape.

I visited my father and mother. She was not in good health, but her spirit was raised by seeing me again. Wheelchair bound, she looked pale and had lost more weight. My father was totally dedicated to her. It made me feel guilty that I couldn't do anything more for her. Except when it came to my grandfather's house.

"I know your granddad is leaving the old house to me in his will," my father explained. "I plan to sell it and split the money three ways between you, your brother and me."

"No, keep my share," I told him. "Put it towards mum's nursing care."

"It'll be a great help to you," my father insisted.

"No, I'll get by."

We left it there.

Over a whisky in the familiar floral wallpapered living room of my parents' home, adorned with ornaments on shelves, I told him of my unearthly experiences at the house and gave him grandfather's diary to read. When he'd finished, he stared ahead in deep thought.

"Interesting," he said after a while, closing the diary.

"Is that all you have to say?" I was shocked and surprised by his reaction.

"I know exactly what happened. It's true your grandfather was forced into helping his sister." He stared into the distance again, as if there was something else he wanted to say, but remained silent, handing the diary back to me. I told him grandfather wanted me to inform the authorities.

"You do as you think fit," he replied. "As far as I'm concerned it's history. Grandchildren often get on better with their grandparents, than children with their own parents."

With that he dropped the subject, leaving me wondering about another family story which I'd probably never know.

Maybe my grandfather's guilt had strained his relationship with my father when he was growing up.

In the fortnight leading up to the funeral, the sadness was eased a little by visiting friends and the freedom of just being able to go to the pub, see a movie, and generally not being tied to a rigid routine of duty. But behind all that was a prevailing sense of loneliness. I missed Marcia's company. I rang her a few times and we chatted about things we'd been doing. I wanted to tell her how much I missed her, but couldn't find the words. I was still unsure of her feelings for me beyond just friendship.

All the while I continued to wrestle with the decision of informing the police and handing over the diary. No-one could harm my grandfather now, and it would only be right for the unfortunate souls, only bones by now I imagined, to be retrieved and given proper burials. Even Emily. Despite my grandfather's understandable wish for her to be in the depths of hell. If there was a life beyond the shadows of ghosts, hopefully it would be more forgiving for all our sakes.

However, one obstacle remained standing in the way of a final decision, and that was Marcia.

On the day of the funeral I left early for the drive to the church. Marcia had generously offered her house to hold the wake after the service. I was deeply impressed by the large turnout of villagers for the occasion.

Marcia was there elegantly dressed in a long black dress and hat, my father beside me as the coffin was lowered into the ground. I couldn't be sure, but I thought I saw someone familiar standing a short distance away behind the assembled mourners. Was it my grandfather smiling at me? Perhaps a trick of the light. As I blinked the image was gone.

My father had to leave after the service to get back to my mother, and with Marcia as host back at the house, I was regaled with stories by the villagers of what a wonderful man grandfather had been. When everyone had left, Marcia invited me to stay the night.

"Your room's ready if you want to," she said. I was grateful for the offer. It had been an emotionally tiring day.

Together we cleared up the plates and glasses left by the guests, then stopped for a break, pouring some wine left over from the wake and resting back on the kitchen counter.

"I'm still trying to make a decision about releasing the diary," I told her.

"Why not?" she asked. "It's your grandfather's wish."

"I know, but I'm worried about you."

"Me? Why?"

"When I hand over the diary to police, there's likely to be a lot of publicity around removing the well capping and searching the waters for remains," I explained.

"Are you sure they'll take the diary seriously? They might think your grandfather made it all up," Marcia didn't seem convinced.

"I'm sure there are past records of those disappearances from the house. They'll probably start putting two and two together."

Marcia accepted the reasoning.

"So why are you concerned about me?" she asked.

"Well I've been staying here, and I know from looks and comments made by the milkman and postman that the locals think our relationship is more than..." I paused, feeling a bit embarrassed to finish the obvious sentence, "... that it's more intimate than it really is. The publicity will associate me with you, and you'll become the gossip of locals. I don't want your reputation as the local doctor to suffer."

Marcia gave me a stony look.

"And you, of course, like the Prince of Knaves will run off back to London and leave me to face them all alone," she angrily accused. I felt terrible. Then she broke into laughter.

"Don't worry yourself, it would take a lot more than that to stop me working here," she said with iron determination. Relief swept over me. I'd have felt totally lost if she really had been casting me out in anger.

"Talking of London," I said, "I've been wondering about a change in my life."

"A change?" Marcia sounded intrigued.

"I was wondering if that position coming up with the local solicitor is still a possible option?"

"You want to live in this area? Surely not in your grandfather's house?"

"No. I never want to go in that place again." The thought chilled me.

"Well yes, the job is still open. Can't guarantee it for you though, but I'm sure you'd stand a good chance. If not, I'm certain you could find work elsewhere in the town."

"Maybe I could start looking for somewhere to live in the area sometime soon," I said, "and if you wanted, we could keep on seeing each other."

"And maybe if you stayed here, we could really give the locals something to gossip about," Marcia smiled.

We kissed, taking the first step together on that uncharted journey ahead.

****

REVELATION

IT was nearly a year later before I learned the results of the police investigation into the remains found at the bottom of the old well.

They were pieced together revealing the bones of three women and a man. That was strange, because I thought there would be the remains of four women. The governess, Victoria, the mother Vera, and Emily. And none of the three women's skeletons showed evidence of rib cage wounds inflicted by gunfire, which would surely have been evident from when my grandfather shot Emily in the chest.

Did he actually shoot her? What happened to her if she wasn't in the well? Did she just leave and never return as my grandfather had first told me?

My father was always tight lipped about his relationship with my grandfather. Was that because he knew the truth?

It was a mystery that continued to vex me, so I contacted my father to try and see if he could shed any light.

At this time Marcia and I were soon to marry, and I'd got the job with the local solicitor who was looking for a new business partner.

My father was reluctant to talk about the past, but agreed to meet me at his house in London. I put the mystery to him as we sat in the living room with cups of tea. My mother was resting in a bedroom along the corridor.

"I'll talk to you about it now," he said, "but afterwards I never want to hear a word about that past again." I agreed to his wish.

"Emily did decide to leave before the marriage," he explained. "Stayed somewhere in the north with an aunt for a number of years. Then one day she returned to the house and obstinately said she was going to stay. I was six years old at the time." He took a sip of tea.

"My mother by now knew the terror that Emily had forced upon my father, and decided to do what he could never have brought himself to do. Later that day I was playing a ball game with Emily in the garden when my mother approached and ordered her to leave. Of course, domineering as ever, she told my mother where to go." A troubled frown formed on my father's face.

"Furious at being insulted, my mother went back into the house and returned a few minutes later holding a shotgun, warning Emily to leave immediately. Once again Emily threw more insults at her and defied her to use the gun. At that moment my father came rushing out the house towards them trying to defuse the situation. But my mother raised the weapon, and in the next second it blasted. Emily flew backwards, falling dead on the lawn."

My father lowered his head, recalling the drama.

"Imagine what it felt like for me as a boy to see the woman shot before my eyes."

He fell silent for minute before continuing, his mind locked in traumatic memory.

"I think your grandfather told you he'd named himself in the diary as being Emily's killer in order to protect his wife's reputation, should the incident ever be investigated. I know that he was greatly relieved when Emily was no more."

"Then what happened to Emily's body?" I asked. "There was nothing to show she was thrown into the old well."

My father appeared to hesitate in answering the question, but finally spoke.

"The well had been capped by then. She's buried under the floorboards in that room where you stayed as a boy." He paused, his eyes rounding on me. "And you are never to tell the police or anyone else. It's a family secret and should stay buried forever."

The shadow of Emily, it seemed, would always remain with me. A family secret to carry to my own grave.

OTHER NOVELS

I hope you enjoyed *Emily's Evil Ghost*. If you would like to read more of my books they are listed at the end and available through Amazon. But first a taste from another of my supernatural novels:

CURSED SOULS GUEST HOUSE

IT BEGAN with the prospect of a great summertime holiday in beautiful countryside. It descended into the jaws of hell.

"The Yorkshire Dales, that's where we should go," my wife Helen suggested as we sat together on the sofa in our two-bedroom apartment. She was flipping through pages of a country living magazine, and had opened a page showing outstanding views of rolling green pastures, hills and dales in the lush rural setting.

The photos were a welcoming sight compared to the outlook from our home in Birmingham, overlooking an endlessly busy main road at the front and an industrial estate at the back.

We had a week's summer holiday coming, and had been wondering how to spend the time.

"Well, what do you think Andrew?" she asked, as I looked across at the magazine photos.

"Looks good," I replied, distracted from watching a nature programme on the TV about tigers. "Don't think we'll meet too many of them in the Dales," I said, pointing to the shot of a tiger leaping at a terrified wild boar trying desperately to escape.

At that moment I didn't realise we too would soon become the victims of a terrifying powerful force intent on our destruction, with cunning far beyond any tiger.

"Be serious," Helen slapped me on the shoulder. "Stop watching the television and concentrate," she commanded. "I'm trying to arrange our holiday. Now I think we should do it as a hiking tour."

"Not sure about hiking. I want to rest on holiday. We can see places in the car." The idea of walking miles was not particularly appealing to me.

"You've become overweight since you got the office manager's job at Mason's Engineering. You need to lose some." Helen had mentioned my increasing size before. I realised the hiking idea was a bit of a ruse she'd been working on for a while.

It was alright for her as an instructor at the local keep fit centre, where we'd first met a few years ago. I was admittedly a lot shapelier then, enjoying regular exercise. Being office bound in a couple of jobs since had changed my lifestyle.

"Okay, we'll do a hiking holiday," I relented. Helen smiled, acknowledging my defeat.

A fortnight later we set off for Carnswold village in the Yorkshire Dales, complete with new shorts, tops, backpacks and hiking boots, heading towards bed and breakfast accommodation which Helen had booked as the base for our week stay.

The route I drove narrowed into hedgerow lined country lanes as we neared the property that would serve as our temporary home. Breaks in the hedges gave views across miles of pastures. Farmsteads and cottages dotted across the plain rose in and out of valleys to the hazy horizon.

The road descended along winding bends with woodland on each side, and crossed a river bridge as we entered a small hamlet lined with stone cottages. The road continued a little further alongside the river until we arrived at Sunny-side, the name of our cottage accommodation.

It was a name to fit the surroundings perfectly. Warm sunshine lighting the field on the other side of the sparkling river, and woodland at the top of a hill beyond. The world seemed restfully peaceful.

The enchantment didn't last long.

Carrying our suitcases from the car, we opened the gate on to a small paved front garden and rang the doorbell. A middle-aged woman with a droopy face answered.

"Mrs Meadows?" I asked. She nodded.

"I'm Andrew Swanson and this is my wife Helen."

"You're early," she snapped.

I looked at my watch. We'd arrived half-an-hour earlier than the three o'clock time of arrival Helen had given in the booking.

"I don't know if your room's ready yet. Wait a minute." She closed the door and left us standing outside.

"Great start," I remarked to Helen.

"Give it a minute," she replied, forever the mediator. "We've probably caught her in the middle of getting things ready for guests."

That I could forgive, but the woman's rudeness annoyed me. Several minutes later the door opened again.

"Come on in then," Mrs Meadows waved her head for us to enter. She led us down a gloomy narrow hallway, bearing faded floral wallpaper, to a desk where we signed in.

"Number five on the first floor," our host barked, handing over the keys. "Dinner's at seven thirty," the woman turned and walked away, entering a room further down the hall and closing the door.

I was unaware Helen had booked an evening meal for us as well, but some food laid on in the evening after a long hike seemed a good idea.

Our room looked drab, a deeply scratched chest of drawers, the wardrobe with a door that didn't close properly and bedside tables that wobbled. The en-suite sink was stained and the shower cubicle hadn't been cleaned.

"Let's try and make the best of it," Helen detected my discontent.

So making the best of it, we spent time taking a riverbank stroll into Carnswold village a short distance away. I saw a pub and suggested I wouldn't mind a holiday pint of beer. The suggestion was met with disapproval.

"No," said Helen, "on this holiday you can have tea, coffee, water and soft drinks. Maybe a glass of wine with evening meals if you're good. You're going to get some of that weight off."

Once again I conceded, and we settled on coffee in a cafe a little way along the narrow cottage lined high street, passing a small sub-post office and newsagent on the way.

After coffee and sandwiches for our late lunch, we continued the stroll down a footpath leading into a wood and out across a field, enjoying the sunshine and relaxation before returning to the unwelcoming lodging for dinner.

The meal was awful. I had beef casserole, which possibly contained the rubbery meat of a cow three hundred years old, and Helen's vegetarian sausages resembled compacted sawdust. Tasted like it too, Helen remarked, pushing them aside on the plate with her fork to attempt the pulp of remaining mashed potato and cabbage.

We looked across at a couple of dinner guests also staying at Sunnyside. Their grim faces showed signs of agreement.

After so called dinner we decided on an early night to be fit and ready for our trekking. Helen looked beautiful as she undressed, her lovely soft face and long, light brown hair, was a familiar sight to me in our everyday routine at home, but in new surroundings my feelings of desire seemed to be newly sparked into life.

"I'm so glad we met," I told her, undressing and approaching. She looked lovingly into my eyes. We kissed and slowly descended on to the bed.

"Aaagh!" she cried, pushing me away just as her back settled on the mattress.

"What?"

"There's a bloody great lump in the bed." Helen rolled to one side and pulled back the quilt. Sure enough, a bed spring from the innards beneath the sheet rose like a small hill in the centre. It was certainly an effective passion dampener, perhaps left like it by the joyless guest house owner I thought.

We settled instead on trying to get a good night's sleep, which wasn't easy, sinking into sagging mattress on either side of the spring. We'd chosen the Yorkshire Dales for its hills and valleys, but hadn't expected to find them in our bed. I was not going to tolerate this place for much longer.

In the morning breakfast was served to us by a man we hadn't seen until now. I presumed he was Mrs Meadows' husband. His drooping face and similar age certainly matched hers. Without greeting he slapped down our breakfasts on the table, bacon and egg for me and a bowl of muesli for Helen, devoid of any other eating choice.

I complained to him about the room and the bed.

"This isn't the bloody Ritz you know," he growled in return. Then stormed out mumbling curses under his breath.

"He's right there," I said to Helen.

"We'll buy some food out," she tried to placate me. "We'll be hiking most of the time. Let's enjoy the daytimes."

Setting off for our first hike, annoyances with the accommodation soon melted away as we crossed amazing countryside, passing sheep, cows and horses grazing in lush meadows.

We'd been hiking for a couple of hours when the footpath led us off a field into a narrow lane. A few hundred yards further up the slope of the lane, we came alongside a high black wrought iron gate, tall red-brick walls stretching away on each side.

The name 'Longhurst House' was embedded in gold lettering on a grey plate set in the sidewall. Through the gate railings we could see a wide gravel forecourt, and beyond a magnificent L-shaped three-storey house with bay windows, crowned by a lantern roof at the corner and gables on each side. We stopped to admire it.

"That place must be very old," I remarked to Helen.

"Some parts of it date back to the 1650s," a woman's voice seemed for a moment to come from nowhere. "It's been extended and rebuilt over the years."

The voice took the form of an elderly woman who appeared from behind the side wall to greet us with a smile through the gate railings.

"Would you like to take a closer look at the house?" she invited, inquisitive eyes set in a wrinkled, kindly face. We nodded that we would.

Wearing gardening gloves, she lifted the latch in the middle of the gate and opened one side. We entered.

The woman had a green apron over her black dress. She removed the gloves and tucked them into the apron's broad front pocket.

"Just doing a bit of gardening," she said. A grass verge with a colourful flowerbed behind ran along one side of the gravel forecourt. On the other side, a lawn split by a paved path fronted the entrance to the house. The red-brick wall, at least fifteen feet high, surrounded the property.

"My family's lived in this house for three generations," the woman told us with pride. "Come and take a look inside if you wish." She led us along the path towards the front door.

"On a hiking holiday are you?" she obviously guessed from our clothing.

"Attempting to get my husband fit again," Helen joked. The woman smiled.

"Silly me, I'm forgetting my manners. I'm Millicent Hendry," the lady introduced herself as we reached the door. "My friends call me Millie, not that I have so many of them now as most of them have died with the passing years. Feel free to call me Millie."

In return I introduced Helen and myself.

Millie opened the sturdy wooden door and beckoned us inside. The entrance hall looked majestic, painted in deep dark red, with ornate coving and half-length wood panelling along the walls. She opened a door into the lounge displaying framed paintings of scenic Yorkshire Dales pastures, a carved wood surround fireplace and valuable looking Georgian chairs.

Another door opened into the lounge, also featuring a carved wood surround fireplace, a large oriental rug, brown leather sofa and a couple of armchairs. More scenic paintings hung on the walls.

At the end of the hallway a glass panelled door looked over the back garden, another wide gravelled area bordered by beds of shrubs and colourful flowers. A door to the side opened on to the kitchen, which was in complete contrast to the traditional setting we'd seen so far. Inside was a modern cooking range, cupboards and work surfaces.

"Health and Safety laws and all that," Millie said apologetically, noticing our surprise at the difference in style. "I used to do bed and breakfast. The old kitchen, flagstone floor, larder and wood burning stove couldn't meet modern legal standards. So a lot of the original has been replaced or covered over for some years now."

Helen and I shook our heads sympathising at Millie's sad parting with the past.

"Pity you don't do bed and breakfast now," I said, lamenting the fact that such a friendly person and wonderful place was unavailable as an alternative to the dump guest house where we were lodging. As I said it, Helen discreetly tugged my arm as if she wanted me to stop going further down that line.

"Well I get the occasional hikers calling to ask if bed and breakfast is available here," Millie replied. "If I like the look of them, sometimes I'm prepared to put them up for a while. Gives me a bit of company since my husband passed away ten years ago."

"I suppose we'd better be making our way back now," said Helen. "We've more walking to do before we return to our lodging and freshen up for dinner."

It was not exactly a welcoming prospect returning to Sunnyside, and heaven knows what foul food awaited for our evening meal, but Helen was right. As we made our way back to the front door, I told Millie about the terrible place where we were staying. We left the house and began walking along the garden path to the forecourt.

"In no way would I wish to interfere with your plans, but if you like, you're very welcome to come and stay here with me for the rest of your holiday," Millie offered. "I can provide breakfast and evening meals, and I have a lovely bedroom that I think you'd find very comfortable."

For me that seemed like an offer we couldn't refuse. Helen's less than enthusiastic face didn't appear so keen.

"Well, we've paid for the place where we're staying," she said. That was true. Because we'd booked at short notice we had to pay full price up front.

"We'll go back and demand a refund," I insisted, turning to Helen. "The place just isn't up to standard for the money."

"I didn't want to cause an argument," Millie intervened. "It wasn't my intention to interfere with your plans."

"You're not. Please don't apologise," I assured her. "I think Helen's just worried about running costs up." My wife gave me a thunderous look as I spoke.

"I'd enjoy your company, that would be enough compensation for the accommodation," said Millie. "My only charge would be for your food, and I can source that at low cost from a local supplier who I've known for years."

I was sold on the offer. Helen seemed to reluctantly agree.

"We'll stay one more night at our lodging and come over to you tomorrow morning if that's okay?" I asked to Millie.

"Perfectly fine," she agreed.

As we stood talking on the forecourt, a man appeared at the open gate holding two alsatians on leads. The dogs saw us and started barking aggressively.

"Quiet!" Millie ordered, with amazing forceful authority for a woman of her age it seemed to me. The animals immediately obeyed, looking almost guilty for making a noise.

"Those are my precious dogs, Rufus and Petra," Millie announced.

The man holding them on the leashes closed the gate behind him and released the animals. They ran to Millie and she bent down to stroke them The dogs looked thrilled to be in the company of their mistress.

Helen grabbed my arm. She was nervous of strange dogs, and large ones like alsatians in particular. A dog had attacked her when she was a girl she'd told me. It left an indelible fear in her psyche. I put my arm round her shoulders to reassure her all was well. Millie noticed Helen's reaction.

"It's okay. They won't hurt you," she added to my reassurance. "They are very obedient, and they know any guests of mine are my friends to be treated with the utmost respect."

As the dogs wandered off towards the back garden, the man who'd brought them here drew near.

"This is my grandson Nicholas, or Nick as we call him," Millie introduced the newcomer. The man was huge. Tall, muscular and wide, wearing a light blue short-sleeved shirt, and navy trousers.

He nodded to our presence saying nothing, just studying us through curious wide eyes set in a large square face, topped by black curly hair.

"Nick takes the alsatians for a walk now and then," Millie continued telling us about her grandson. "And to dog training sessions every Saturday morning in the village, don't you Nick?" she prompted. The man nodded again. It appeared he was not a great talker.

"There's some homemade blackberry and apple crumble in the kitchen I've made for you," she told him. The news brought a smile to the man's face. He left, heading into the house.

"Forgive Nick, he doesn't say much, but has a heart of gold," Millie explained. "His mother, my daughter, and her husband died in a tragic car crash when he was a boy. I don't think he's ever truly got over the trauma. I brought him up and now he leads a fairly independent life working for a local builder. He has a flat in Oxton village a couple of miles away."

Helen and I weren't quite sure how to respond. It was such a sad tale. Millie saw our awkwardness.

"You're on holiday. Don't let me weigh you down with long past family woes," she brightened up with a smile. "Shall I see you tomorrow?"

"Definitely," I replied. Helen gave a half-hearted nod.

"I think you'll have a truly memorable time here," said Millie, as we walked towards the gate to leave. In the event, she was truly right.

Making our way back across the pastures to Sunnyside, I asked Helen why she'd tugged my arm when Millie suggested we could stay at her house.

"I don't know," she replied, "just this feeling about the place came over me."

"But Millie's a lovely lady," I said. "It looks a fantastic place compared to the rat hole we're staying in. Good deal on the cost too."

"I know, I know," Helen agreed. "Just a feeling I have, that's all."

Soon Andrew and Helen discover that Millie's welcome greeting hides a horrifying plot.

Find out what happens next.

CURSED SOULS GUEST HOUSE

Available on Amazon

MORE BOOKS BY THE AUTHOR

DEAD SPIRITS FARM

An abandoned old farmhouse turns into a couple's haunted nightmare.

DEADLY ISLAND RETREAT

Trapped on a remote island with ghosts and horrifying revelations.

DARK SECRETS COTTAGE

Shocking family secrets unearthed in a haunted cottage.

THE BEATRICE CURSE

Burned at the stake, a witch returns to wreak revenge.

THE BEATRICE CURSE 2

Sequel to the Beatrice Curse

THE SOUL SCREAMS MURDER

A family faces terror in a haunted house.

A GHOST TO WATCH OVER ME

A ghostly encounter exposes horrific revelations.

A FRACTURE IN DAYBREAK

A family saga of crime, love and dramatic reckoning.

VENGEANCE ALWAYS DELIVERS

When a stranger calls – revenge strikes in a gift of riches.

THE ANARCHY SCROLL

A perilous race to save the world in a dangerous lost land.

All available on Amazon

For more information or if you have any questions please email me:

geoffsleight@gmail.com

Or visit my Amazon Author page:

www.amazon.com/Geoffrey-Sleight

Tweet: twitter.com/resteasily

Printed in Great Britain
by Amazon